The Elusive Young Lady

When Lord Bartram Stanwood first met Theodosia Elston, the young lady seemed a model of sober respectability and plain-dressed propriety.

Yet when she came with Bartram's flighty sister for a stay at the estate of Stanwood Oaks, Theo appeared as a dazzlingly sophisticated lady of fashion.

Even more bewildering, the viscount witnessed her outrageous behavior in the arms of eager gentlemen in the ballroom. And then again on the back of his most fiery mount, skimming fences in the fields. He therefore could hardly be faulted for thinking her a female as heedless as a child and as shocking as a scarlet woman.

Lord Bartram definitely had to find out who the real Theo was—before he fell in love with the wrong one. . . .

THE CHARMING IMPOSTOR

SIGNET Regency Romances You'll Want to Read

THE CHARMING IMPOSTOR

APRIL KIHLSTROM

A SIGNET BOOK

NEW AMERICAN LIBRARY

SIGNET TRADEMARK REG. U.S.PAT.OFF. AND FOREIGN COUNTRIES
REGISTERED TRADEMARK—MARCA REGISTRADA
HECHO EN CHICAGO, U.S.A.

SIGNET, SIGNET CLASSIC, MENTOR, PLUME, MERIDIAN AND NAL BOOKS
are published by New American Library,
1633 Broadway, New York, New York 10019

First Printing, September, 1985

1 2 3 4 5 6 7 8 9

PRINTED IN THE UNITED STATES OF AMERICA

1

"Dosie," you *must* save me or I shall go mad!" said the young lady dressed in somber gray.

She was petite and blond, and even someone who did not know her might have guessed that her dress had been chosen by a chaperon more concerned with the proprieties of mourning than the dictates of fashion.

Theodosia Elston, who was a tall, slender, dark-haired beauty, regarded her dearest friend and laughed as she replied, "I shouldn't, if I were you. Your complexion would be sure to be ruined by a stay in Bedlam."

Miss Helena Stanwood flung herself into the nearest chair and answered crossly, "You ought not to roast me, Dosie. I am persuaded *you* would not like it, either, if you were to find yourself shut up all day. I shall go mad if Cousin Roberta does not allow me to go out riding with you! I cannot bear not to be on horseback. How can that offend anyone? It is not, after all, as though I were asking to go dancing! But my cousin has the most antiquated notions when it comes to mourning. Or to anything else. How I long for the day when I can be back in colors again. And wear something becomingly in the mode. Look at my dress! The sleeves are too short for fashion, the neck too high, and the color abominable compared to your own sprigged muslin. I swear Cousin Roberta is afraid I shall carry on another clandestine affair if she allows me the least freedom of dress or movement."

"Such an absurd fear, of course," Theodosia said dryly. Helena Stanwood had the grace to blush, and Theodosia added thoughtfully, "How unfortunate that your brother will not take your side. Perhaps if he came to Bath and paid a call on your cousin he could prevail upon her to allow you more freedom."

"Well, he will not! He is, he writes, mired in affairs at Stanwood Oaks and cannot leave. Not even to rescue me from desperation!" Helena retorted crossly. "It was bad enough that Mama and Papa sent me here to Bath to live with Papa's cousin and to go to school, but for Bartram to *leave* me in Cousin Roberta's care after they died is unpardonable! Besides, I've no doubt he would agree with Cousin Roberta entirely. He has become insufferably proper in the past year or so."

Ignoring this diatribe that she had heard so often before, Theodosia said, "Well, your year of mourning will be up soon enough, and then your father's cousin must allow you more freedom."

It was Helena's turn to ignore Dosie. Thoughtfully she said, "You know, Cousin Roberta has not seen Bartram for years."

Puzzled, Theodosia asked, "What is that to the point?"

Helena considered the matter. "Papa always brought me to Bath himself, and the few times she visited us at home, my brother was never there. And Bartram wrote the news that Mama and Papa were dead—he didn't come himself to tell us. And as I had so nonsensically contracted the flu, it was out of the question for us to travel to attend the funeral."

Suddenly awareness overwhelmed Theodosia. "No, Nella! You cannot mean what I fear you mean!"

Helena smiled demurely. "And what is that?" she teased her friend.

"You know very well," Theodosia retorted severely. "You mean for me to come calling as your brother, don't you?"

Helena grinned. "If *your* brother's clothes still fit you, why not? You may not be kept quite as close as I am, but Bath must still be unbearably quiet to you. Why shouldn't we kick up a lark? No one would ever guess it was you. And Bartram is safely ensconced back at Stanwood Oaks, so there is no risk of exposure. You need only take me for an afternoon ride and then I swear I shall find my imprisonment possible to bear!"

Theodosia hesitated, and Helena pressed her further. "When you played Hamlet at Mrs. Plimpton's Academy, no one would have guessed you were a girl had they not already known it. I don't know whether it was your height or the way you brushed back your hair or your manners when you dressed as Hamlet, but I swear it was amazing!"

"And what of your cousin's servants?" Theodosia flung back at her. "It is all very well to talk of fooling your cousin, because she is, after all, nearsighted. But they are not, and they see me almost every day. One of them is certain to recognize me."

"What of it?" Helena countered. "You know they are loyal to me and think Cousin Roberta far too strict! I swear they will not betray us. If I am asked, I shall simply tell them it is all for a lark. Which it is. Oh, Dosie, please say you will do it."

"So long as I take care to remain in dim light," Theodosia mused quietly, "we might get away with it." She looked at her friend's face and read the very real desperation there. "Very well," she said reluctantly, "we shall do it. *If* George's clothes still fit me. And here is the part you must do to help, Nella. . . ."

The young man who presented himself to the house of Miss Roberta Stanwood was, in that lady's eyes, a most estimable fellow. A trifle younger than she had expected, perhaps, but then, her eyesight *was* failing and certainly there was nothing to cavil at in his manners. He was dressed impeccably in a riding coat of russet and breeches of a delicate biscuit color. His boots were nicely polished and his cravat discreetly arranged. As for his dark hair, it curled more than was perhaps fashionable, but on this young man it looked quite well. Certainly Miss Helena Stanwood thought so.

"Bartram!" she cried as she saw him standing beside her cousin in the drawing room. "How wonderful to see you!"

The Viscount Stanwood held his sister at arm's length and studied her carefully for a moment. "You've grown up, Nella," he said gravely. "Not taller, but then, we do not look for that, since Mama was short, but more of a lady, to be sure. And your hair! I had no notion you had become so fashionable."

Miss Roberta Stanwood regarded her young cousin Helena with satisfaction. The girl was modestly attired in lavender, Roberta having made her this concession to the coming end of the first year of mourning. And in spite of the viscount's words, Helena's blond hair was dressed to the back of her head in a manner that would not draw attention to her. A pity the viscount was already so thoroughly out of mourning, but then, gentlemen were allowed more latitude in such matters. Miss Stanwood was dressed, herself, in the black she had taken up years before, upon her own parents' death, and never abandoned.

A few more minutes of polite conversation passed and then the viscount said, a trifle anxiously, "You look rather pale, Nella. Perhaps a ride would do you good. Cousin Roberta, I am sure you will excuse us while I take my sister out for some air?"

"Of course," Miss Stanwood replied, her heart touched by this evidence of brotherly solicitude. "But the hour is a trifle late. Should you not wait until tomorrow?"

The viscount regarded her cousin gravely. "Perhaps. But I must be off this very night, back to my estate."

Miss Stanwood could find nothing to say to that, so Miss Helena hurried upstairs to change to her riding habit. The viscount made polite conversation with Miss Stanwood, who could not entirely repress a sigh of relief that everything was going so well. She had rather dreaded meeting the new viscount and telling him some of the things that had occurred before she decided to keep Helena so confined. But Bartram really did seem to be an amiable young fellow, and surely he would *not* hold her to blame.

So amiable was he that when the viscount and his sister had gone, Miss Roberta Stanwood headed for the kitchen to consult with the cook just what they could serve the viscount for refreshment when he returned from his ride. She was most anxious that he should be sent on his way in continued good spirits!

2

The Viscount Bartram Stanwood was tired. He had been traveling most of the day and would gladly have stopped for the night at the last cozy inn he had passed. Unfortunately, he could not. He had decided to visit his sister, Helena, in Bath, and visit her he would. Never mind that he was, at this rate, likely to arrive at a decidedly shabby hour; surely even his father's prim cousin Roberta would understand the difficulties of pressing a horse for speed when it has thrown out a splint. And if she did not, she would nevertheless hold her tongue, for Bartram was the one paying her expenses as chaperon to Helena.

As the coach jolted him one more time, the viscount sighed. That was another source of his poor temper. He would far prefer to have driven his curricle or ridden on horseback, and indeed had planned to do so. At the last moment, however, upon impulse, he had chosen to use the family traveling coach. His sister's last letter had indicated a restlessness he could not help but sympathize with, and it was in his mind to perhaps bring her back to Stanwood Oaks with him. She would have liked nothing better than to travel in his curricle, Stanwood knew, but that was a journey he would prefer not to make. If she came with him, she would ride in the traveling carriage, as was only proper for a young lady, and he would ride either with her or on horseback.

A stranger would have called the viscount a remarkably handsome young man, with blond hair brushed *coup-de-vent*, green eyes, and impeccably tailored clothes. If the severity of unrelieved black seemed a trifle strong, the observer nevertheless could not doubt that the viscount wore it most properly for mourning. With a snort Bartram wondered if his sister had yet persuaded Miss Stanwood to allow her out of mourning and into colors. It would be just like her to have done so.

The coach slowed and came to a halt. Surprised, the viscount looked out and saw nothing but countryside. The driver appeared at the door of the coach, coughed, and said, "We be almost at Bath, m'lord, but I'd best ease the pace a bit."

Incredulously the viscount retorted, "What? But we are crawling as it is."

The voice came again. "Aye, but the mare seems to be laboring more'n ever."

"Very well," came the viscount's grudging reply.

It was therefore perhaps not surprising that the Viscount Stanwood arrived at his cousin's

house in Bath in a terrible humor. Nor was it improved by the astonished look the butler gave him when he told the fellow who he was. Indeed Bartram was obliged to speak frostily to the fellow before he would take the viscount's coat and lead him in to Cousin Roberta. "Please inform my cousin I am here," he said. "I realize I am unexpected but trust that the rules of hospitality nevertheless hold true and that my cousin will receive me in spite of the lateness of the hour."

"Y-yes, sir. M'lord. R-right this way, m'lord," the fellow stammered.

Directing one last command to his coachman, the viscount turned and did as he was bid. If he had thought the butler's reaction to his appearance odd, Bartram quickly discovered that it was nothing to his cousin's welcome. Indeed, his first reaction was that he had walked into Bedlam.

"*Bartram?* But where is Helena?" Cousin Roberta quavered. "Aren't you taller now? And wasn't your hair darker?"

The viscount raised his quizzing glass. "My dear cousin," he said coolly, "what the devil are you talking about?"

Nervously her hands fluttered in front of her. "But you came earlier and took Helena out riding. Didn't you? My wretched eyes, no doubt, but I could have sworn you were shorter then."

Angrily tugging off his gloves and tossing them onto a table, Bartram retorted, "Perhaps I was, Cousin Roberta." At her look of astonishment, he went on, "Whatever you are babbling about, it does not concern me. I have only now

arrived, and if some other gentleman came earlier and claimed to be me, he was an impostor."

"B-but Helena *called* him Bartram," Miss Stanwood protested feebly. "How could I have known?"

Grimly the viscount replied, "You could not have. Rest easy, cousin, I acquit you of blame in the matter. It is clear to me that my minx of a sister must have been engaged in a clandestine encounter which involved the fellow posing as me. I have come to Bath just in time, it seems."

Hesitantly Miss Stanwood said, "You do not think they could have eloped, do you?"

For a moment Bartram closed his eyes. "We must hope not. I have no desire for that sort of scandal in the family. But I suppose I shall have to go and look for my wretched sister, just in case she has yielded to such madness. I'd best go tell Peter to arrange for new horses."

As he spoke, however, the viscount turned and saw his sister enter the parlor. She looked very pale but she spoke brightly enough. "Bartram. What a delightful surprise! When did you arrive? How was your journey? How is everything at Stanwood Oaks?"

One hand rested negligently on his hip as Bartram replied, "You are very cool about it, Nella. My compliments. It won't wash, however. You are going to tell me who the young man was, where he took you, and why he felt it necessary to pose as me."

Helena's eyes met her brother's and dropped when she saw the implacable anger in them. She

knew him too well to ignore the warning she saw there. "Very well," she said crossly. "I was tired of always being cooped up here, and my friend agreed to take me out riding."

"Go on," her brother prodded, "I feel sure there is more you can tell me. Such as your friend's name."

"D-Devere," she stammered hastily. "He . . . he only posed as you because he knew Cousin Roberta would not let me go with him otherwise. B-because we are in mourning."

"I see," Bartram said, his mouth grim. "No doubt she may have had other reasons as well? A need to curb a young girl too prone to clandestine encounters, perhaps?"

Helena gasped and looked at Roberta in outrage. With a harsh laugh her brother said, "Do not look at her like that, Nella. Cousin Roberta did not betray you, it was merely an inspired guess on my part. *You* betrayed yourself."

Resolutely Helena squared her shoulders and asked, "What are you going to do about it?"

For a long moment the viscount did not answer. Instead he inspected a minute spot on his impeccably tailored jacket. Finally he looked at her and said in measured tones, "I? I shall take you back to Stanwood Oaks tomorrow. Or rather," he amended after a moment's recollection of the day's journey, "as soon as it is feasible to do so."

"But you cannot!" she protested.

Bartram raised his eyebrows in astonishment. "Cannot?" he said. "It think you forget yourself, Nella. Under Mama and Papa's admittedly slapdash will, *I* am your guardian until you come of age. And I will not permit you to remain here while you are so flighty. Come," he said coaxingly, "what is there to keep you here save some fellow who has not even the decency to behave with propriety toward you? You are finished with your schooling and I cannot believe that Bath society has such allure for you. Particularly when you have been in mourning this past year."

"True," Helena conceded reluctantly. "But my very best friend in the world is here, and I cannot bear to leave her!"

The viscount, it must be said, appeared totally unmoved by this impassioned statement. Coolly he said, "And who is this friend you cannot bear to be parted from? Some hoyden, no doubt."

"That's not fair!" Helena said hotly. "Dosie is perfectly respectable. More than you are, I don't doubt!"

At this point Miss Roberta Stanwood was moved to intervene. "Lady Theodosia Elston *is* quite unexceptionable," she said timidly. "And a most desirable influence on Helena."

If Helena was amused or surprised at this accolade for her friend, she hid it well. Instead she watched her brother, who appeared thoughtful. After a moment he turned to her and said, "I have no wish to figure as an ogre in your eyes, Nella. Would you be more pleased to return with me to Stanwood Oaks if we invited your friend to come as well? And Cousin Roberta to chaperon, of course."

For a moment Helena gaped at her brother; then she threw her arms around his neck. "Would you? Invite her, I mean? Oh, Bartram, I *should* like to see home again, and if Dosie came too, that would make it perfect!"

Gently the viscount detached himself from his sister's enthusiastic embrace. Dryly he said, "The Earl of Elston's family is not noted for its sober, respectable behavior. If, however, when I call upon the girl tomorrow, I find her as Cousin Roberta said, a well-bred young lady likely to exert an improving influence upon you, then we shall indeed invite her to come with us."

Her young mind working feverishly, Helena agreed fervently. "An excellent notion, Bartram. I am persuaded you shall find her as respectable as even you could wish."

"Indeed?" he said thoughtfully. "Then I confess I am hard put to understand why *you* are her friend. I should have thought you would find her a bore."

Shrewdly Helena looked at her brother. In a voice as quiet as his own, she replied, "Do you know, I somehow think that once you see Dosie you will understand perfectly. She *is* respectable but at the same time manages to have such laughing eyes that one cannot believe her to be a bore." At her brother's expression of patent disbelief, Helena shrugged crossly. "Oh, very well, wait and see."

"I shall," was the smooth reply. Then, to Miss Stanwood he added, "Cousin Roberta, I wonder if something might be found in the kitchen for me to eat? I have been traveling all day and confess I could do with some refreshment."

Instantly Miss Roberta was all aflutter with confusion. "Yes, of course. Shall I ring for a tray? No, you would much rather dine at the table, I am sure. But that will not be for another half-hour. . . ."

With a kindness he had not yet shown his sister, the viscount said soothingly, "Please, Cousin Roberta, do not distress yourself. A tray would be perfectly acceptable. Here or in my room or at table, I cannot believe it will affect the taste of the food one jot. However, I assure you that it will take me at least that half-hour to change out of my traveling things, so perhaps it would be as well to simply all dine together."

Pleased to have it all settled so neatly, Cousin Roberta hastily agreed. Helena, equally hastily, said, "I, too, must go change."

Bartram watched her flee the room, perfectly aware of her desire to avoid further questions. At a far more discreet pace he followed her lead. Plenty of time to question his sister at Stanwood Oaks. Meanwhile he would take care to ensure that Nella had no opportunity for further rendez-vous or clandestine correspondence.

3

Lady Theodosia dressed with extreme care. Nella's note had arrived just as she was sipping her morning chocolate, and she knew by the hour that something extraordindary had occurred. To be sure, the note was rather muddled, but Dosie was able to deduce that she was to be at her most respectable today.

Lady Willoughby, upon seeing her granddaughter, remarked conversationally, "Now, I wonder what you are up to this time? Yesterday you slipped in the back way dressed as a boy, and today you appear to have become a Puritan. Do you mean to tell me why?"

Theodosia had long since ceased to be surprised by her grandmother's apparent omniscience. Experience had taught her, moreover, that it was useless to prevaricate. On the other hand, Grandmama was not one to pry. "I think it best that I not tell you," Theodosia answered after a moment's reflection. "At least not beforehand.

You are the best of grandmothers, but even you might feel obliged to intervene."

As if in agreement, Lady Willoughby sighed. "Do you know, Dosie, the most tiresome thing about being a chaperon? One is obliged to try to make one's charge pursue a course of propriety. *I* don't mind if you kick up a lark by dressing as a boy. So long as you are good at it. But as your chaperon I am obliged to warn you that it is not at all the thing and threaten to take away your privileges if you do it again."

Dosie smiled affectionately at her grandmother. Theirs was, most certainly, an unusual family. One that, had it not carried such a venerable title, must have long ago found itself shunned by the rest of the *ton.* But what would have been disgraceful in another was merely charmingly eccentric when done by an Elston. Particularly as no one in the line had ever been offensively eccentric or truly harmed anyone, as had members of other notorious families. And indeed it began to look as if this generation might become positively respectable. Why, look at George. There had been a time when he was ripe for any mischief. But since his marriage and since Papa had died and George had become the new earl, he had become thoroughly upright, even taking it upon himself to lecture Dosie that she ought to begin looking about her for a husband!

Abruptly Lady Willoughby's voice broke into Theodosia's reverie. "I shall be going out this morning. Unless you are expecting visitors?"

With a perfectly grave face Dosie replied, "I

thought I might do some needlework this morning, Grandmama."

"That settles it," Lady Willoughby said grimly. "You *are* up to something. And I must be here to see what it is."

Theodosia's eyes began to dance. "Well, I do think you might enjoy it," she said with a gurgle of laughter. "Nella's brother is in town and means to call on me this morning. A *most* sober and upright fellow, I understand."

Lady Willoughby looked at her granddaughter in disbelief. "Call on you this morning? Surely you cannot mean . . ."

Only then did Theodosia realize how her words had sounded. "No, no," she said hastily. "Not to ask for my hand, as I collect you fear. No," she added, a trifle puzzled herself, "I don't know why he is coming. Nella's note was rather rattled, I'm afraid. But I collect he means to carry her off to the country, and there is something he wishes *me* to do. Go with her, I think, but I cannot conceive why he should want me to do so. At any rate, Nella has bidden me to be at my most respectable."

Lady Willoughby nodded in perfect comprehension. "And you could not bear to keep from going one step further?" she suggested. "My dear girl, one of these days your penchant for the absurd is going to land you in the briars! And if it doesn't, it certainly ought to."

Theodosia merely laughed. "I mean to do no more than make myself agreeable to him and satisfy his desire to find a respectable companion for Nella so that he will invite me to accompany her to the country."

"But why should you wish him to?" her grandmother protested. "Have you grown so tired of my company? And of the amusements here in Bath? Or of Holwell?"

Ignoring the last question, Theodosia reached out to hold her grandmother's hands. "Not tired of you, precisely, merely so . . . so restless. I had just a taste of London society before Maria's doctor decreed that she was too far along in her breeding and must retire to the country. And I was sent back here. You are the dearest of grandmothers, but I find I cannot bear Bath just now."

Dryly her grandmother replied, "Surely you cannot believe that a country estate will be more exciting than Bath? Why, if that were so, you would have accompanied your brother and Maria home."

" 'A young girl *must* not be exposed to such things!' " Theodosia mimicked expertly her sister-in-law's nervous voice. Lady Willoughby laughed sympathetically, and Dosie went on, more seriously now, "I do not crave excitement, Grandmama. Rather, my taste of a Season has made me aware how soon I must curb my exuberance and dance to society's tune. Not a happy picture, and yet what alternative have I? To remain a spinster all my life? I am not made for that. In the country . . . well, in the country there will be fewer eyes to see, and I may perhaps find an outlet for my rashness and clear it all away."

"Under the eyes of this oh-so-sober brother?" Lady Willoughby asked skeptically.

Theodosia caught her lower lip between her teeth. "Well, perhaps he will not always be there, and in any event, the worst *he* can do is pack me off back to Bath. And then I am no worse off than if I had never gone."

Lady Willoughby sighed and shook her head. "So you do wish to whistle Holwell down the wind. I was afraid of that. And yet I cannot entirely blame you." She sighed again, then said resolutely, "Well, I have no doubt you will convince this brother of Nella's to take you to the country with her. I only hope you do not land us all in the briars with your nonsense."

"Because ours is such a sober, respectable family, of course," Dosie countered with mock seriousness.

"Don't remind me," her grandmother said with a sigh, "of all the *on-dits* our family has been the subject of. Particularly not," she added hastily, "my own contribution from my salad days!"

"Why, Grandmama," Theodosia said with mock innocence, "*I* thought your greatest scandal was that you married a *mere* baron after Grandfather died!"

Together they laughed and in mutual good humor retired to the drawing room to wait for Viscount Stanwood to call.

The viscount paused on the steps of the neat little house on the quiet, fashionable street of

Bath. Its very address spoke for the respectability of its inhabitants. Except, the viscount thought grimly, the Elstons were not noted for such things. Nevertheless, he sounded the knocker and displayed nothing but grave courtesy as he gave his card to the butler and requested to see the Lady Theodosia Elston. The fellow bowed and said, equally gravely, "Please follow me."

The viscount did so, his alert eyes taking in everything about the place. And when the door to the drawing room was opened for him he noted approvingly the quiet comfort of its decor. Indeed he was almost moved to smile until his eyes alighted on the younger of the two ladies in the salon, and then he almost gave voice to his astonishment. Nella's friend? Impossible! But then she looked at him, and it was as Nella had said: her eyes were dancing.

Meanwhile Lady Willoughby had come forward to greet him. "The Viscount Stanwood, I believe," she said, holding out her hand to him.

Hastily he made his bow as he replied, "Yes. My sister is, I believe, a friend of your granddaughter's."

"Indeed," Lady Willoughby said a trifle frostily. "A rather flighty young thing. But then, my granddaughter is, I believe, an improving influence on her. Come, Theodosia, and make the gentleman your curtsy."

Choking back a sharp retort, Dosie did as she was bid and murmured a greeting. Lady Willoughby then invited him to sit down, and

Bartram did so. "You have known my sister long?" he asked Theodosia politely.

"For several years," Dosie agreed. "We were at school together, here in Bath."

"And yet you are older, are you not?" he persisted.

"By a year," she agreed, "but at our age it scarcely matters."

"A year," the viscount murmured to himself. "But should you not have been brought out yet? If she were not in mourning, Nella would have made her curtsy to the *ton* this year."

Theodosia hesitated and Lady Willoughby answered for her. "Two years ago my granddaughter was in mourning, sir. *Her* father's death preceded your father's by no more than a year. As for this spring, she was brought out, but family matters required that she retire from the Season until next year."

"I see," the viscount said curtly, a slight sneer curling his mouth. "A scandal, perhaps, or ought not I say that?"

Lady Willoughby visibly bristled and her voice dripped ice as she replied, "Your manners are abominable, sir. Do not judge my granddaughter by the girls *you* know."

Quietly Theodosia added, "It is none of your affair, but my sister-in-law found herself in the family way and her doctor decreed that she retreat to the country, and I was returned here to Bath."

A thoughtful frown creased the viscount's brow. "Why not to your mother?" he asked. "Indeed, why is she not bringing you out in the first place?''

Theodosia went white and her voice was tight with anger as she said, "You fight with the gloves off, don't you, sir? As you surely must be aware, my mother went off to America some years ago. I have made the choice not to follow her."

It was Stanwood's turn to go white. Shaken, he replied, "Forgive me, I had not known. Or if I had known, I had forgotten. I did not mean my visit to be an inquisition."

"Then why are you asking all these questions?" Lady Willoughby asked practically.

Grateful for her sensible manner, Stanwood turned to Lady Willoughby with relief. "I think it best to remove my sister from Bath for a time. To take her back to our country home. She said that your granddaughter was her friend, and I thought perhaps to invite her along. If . . ."

"If she proved acceptable?" Lady Willoughby finished for him. "Unfortunately, I am not at all sure I can give my approval to such a scheme."

"Grandmama!" Theodosia exclaimed.

The viscount was even more outspoken. Rather tightly he asked, "May I ask what you mean?"

Lady Willoughby shrugged and waved her hand about carelessly. "Well, you are unmarried, your mother died with your father, and I cannot see that there would be anyone to chaperon. I cannot allow something which even gives rise to the illusion of impropriety."

Grimly the viscount replied, "There is a house-keeper. Nevertheless, I have no doubt that my father's cousin, Miss Roberta Stanwood, can be prevailed upon to accompany us for as long as we are there. In any event, my fiancée—or rather the woman I hope will become my fiancée—lives on a neighboring estate and will be there to keep an eye on matters from time to time. Surely that would suffice?"

Lady Willoughby hesitated. After a moment she said reluctantly, "I suppose it must. Very well, *if* my granddaughter wishes to go, I shall give my consent."

Stanwood looked expectantly at Theodosia, who was staring at her lap. Without lifting her head she said, "I think perhaps I would."

For a moment the viscount stared at her suspiciously, certain he had heard the sound of laughter in her words. But she continued to stare at her hands and he said gravely, "Thank you. My sister will be pleased to hear it. And now I must be going."

The viscount took his leave feeling almost as though he had escaped from a madhouse. It was perhaps fortunate that he did not hear the laughter that filled the room he left behind.

4

The coach that traveled northward was lined in silk, with comfortable cushions and the best of springs, and carried only two young women. Behind it was a simpler coach hired to carry the trunks and boxes of the two young women, as well as their chaperon, who declared she preferred to be alone. Beside these coaches rode a handsome figure of a man, and only someone as uncivil as his sister would have wondered that he chose to sit on horseback on such a fine day rather than ride inside with her.

But protest Helena did. "It is so uncivil toward *you*, Dosie! As though your comfort mattered not in the least."

Lady Theodosia smiled tranquilly. "Come now, Nella, even you cannot say this coach is uncomfortable! How can he afford it when you say the estate is run straight into the ground?"

Crossly her friend replied, "He did not. Bartram would never bring himself to *waste* his blunt on such a fine carriage. Mama and Papa bought it just a few weeks before they drowned. If it didn't have the family emblem on it, Bartram would no doubt have sold it ages ago!" she concluded spitefully.

Theodosia laughed. "Well, then, we must be grateful that he could not." She paused and watched him through the windows of the coach. After a moment she sighed. "I must admit, however, that I envy him the right to ride outside on horseback. I should love to gallop, rather than being cooped up in here!"

"When we get to Stanwood Oaks, you shall have as many gallops as you wish," her friend vowed fervently. "And I shall join you!"

Spoken in just that tone, with the flash of fire in her eyes, Nella's words might well have been taken as a challenge. Theodosia, however, was content to nod her head. Given Nella's impulsive nature, headlong gallops about the countryside were probably the safest outlet for her rebelliousness. Aloud she said, "Just so long as Devere need not appear!"

Helena giggled most improperly. "Bartram was *so* angry," she said. "And I vow that not one of the servants gave him the least hint who it was —even if they knew. Admit it: it *was* the greatest of larks."

Reluctantly Theodosia grinned, and Helena crowed triumphantly. "And to think my brother finds you the most respectable young lady he has ever seen!" she said.

Theodosia blinked in disbelief. "He cannot have said that," she protested.

"But he did. And told me I must school myself to be more like you," Helena assured her solemnly.

This time it was Theodosia who could not keep from laughing outright. "How fortunate," she gasped, "that he has never seen Devere!"

Helena laughed. "Do you know, he is in such charity with me for having such a respectable friend that he has even agreed to allow me to come out of mourning and into colors once we are in the country?"

"You cannot mean it!" Theodosia retorted, awed. "It is still one week short of a year."

Solemnly Helena nodded. "But he does mean it. In return I am to model myself upon you."

Once again both friends dissolved into laughter. When they had stopped, however, Helena turned serious. "Are you sorry to be leaving Holwell behind?"

Abruptly Theodosia was sober. "No," she said quietly, "I think I shall be better for a time away from him."

"But he has money, breeding, and is devoted to you. He followed you down from London when you came back to Bath, and I could swear that any day he would have come up to scratch. *I* think it would be rather nice to marry someone with lots and lots of money so that one need never count pennies."

Theodosia turned her head away. "I have money," she said with some constraint. "And it is precisely because I felt Holwell was about to propose that I was grateful to accept your brother's invitation to accompany you to the Oaks. When I think of marriage, I think of being trapped, not of being free."

"When I think of marriage," Helena countered, "I think of having as much pin money as I want and all the rights of a young matron. We could go where we pleased, when we pleased, without a footman trailing behind us and no one to ask where we'd been."

"Except perhaps our husbands," Theodosia pointed out dryly.

"Oh, fustian! Must you be such a pessimist?" Helena complained.

Dosie grinned and made peace with her friend.

Outside the coach, Viscount Stanwood was, as usual, running figures through his head. After almost a year he had finally begun to get the estate on a decent footing, but no matter how he considered matters, he could not see how to provide a Season for Nella, nor even a dowry if some gentleman did ask her to marry him. And yet she must have her chance!

That led his thoughts to Miss Cranley. *Her* father was well-heeled and had thrown out hints more than once that Stanwood's title well outweighed his lack of funds in making him an acceptable suitor. Miss Cranley was, moreover, unquestionably proper, and Bartram could not doubt she had been well schooled in how to run a household. Just the sort of woman his mother had not been. There was no question that the estate showed the years of neglect by a mistress who cared more about clothes and baubles than about anything else. Swallowing hard, Bartram found himself thinking that Miss Cranley was just the sort of wife he ought to have. Why, then, did he find it so hard to formalize the matter?

Resolutely the viscount shook his head. It was of far more importance to ensure that his sister was content to stay quietly at Stanwood Oaks until he *could* send her to London for a Season. Surely Lady Theodosia's presence would help. How surprising to find a member of *that* family so sensible and sober. Though her traveling clothes had seemed far more fashionable than those she had worn when he called upon her in Bath, it did not occur to Stanwood to wonder what else might be different.

The journey, while a long one, passed pleasantly enough, and Stanwood was all quiet courtesy toward his charges at the inn they stopped at for the night. Indeed he even kept them company in the private parlor after dinner, and it was there that Cousin Roberta astonished her listeners. She interrupted the conversation rather abruptly by saying, "Do you know, Bartram, your grandfather, *my* uncle, never really trusted your father. He was fond of saying that his son would run the estate right into the ground. Which he did. Said he was going to make a provision for you. Funds or something to be hidden where your father couldn't touch it. Did you ever find it? Your inheritance, I mean?"

For the briefest moment Bartram Stanwood considered the possibility that his cousin was in her cups. But then he recalled that she had not even touched the wine served with dinner, and a more disturbing suggestion presented itself. With the care he might have used with someone on her way to Bedlam, Bartram said, "No, Cousin Roberta, I have not. But then, I had no notion there was anything to look for. Surely the lawyers would have told me if there were."

Cousin Roberta smiled condescendingly. "You never knew your grandfather. Died when you were a few days old. He didn't like lawyers. Didn't like the fact the estate was entailed and he couldn't leave it anywhere but to his son, even if that wasn't a very satisfactory child. Left the necessary papers to be found by the first male descendant smart enough to find them. And that's who would get his inheritance."

With precisely the sort of bluntness her relatives were always deprecating in her, Nella said, "Yes, but why did he tell *you* all this? Why didn't he leave any clues for *us?*"

Rather proudly Cousin Roberta looked at her. "I am the clue. I was to tell the grandchildren precisely on the first anniversary of his son's death. But tonight seemed more appropriate. As for why he told me, well, your grandfather always liked me. He always hated the fact your father and I were so closely related, for otherwise he would have wanted an alliance between us. Perhaps that is why I have never been very welcome at the Oaks since your grandfather died: jealousy on the part of your mother, Stanwood. *She* knew the attraction your father and I had for one another. But I would never have told him about your grandfather's treasure, for your grandfather didn't want me to. *I* knew his wishes perfectly well."

For several moments there was a stunned silence as Bartram and his sister tried to picture Cousin Roberta as their mother. It was Theodosia who came to the rescue by saying in a quiet, calm voice, "I do recall that such things were briefly fashionable thirty years ago—at least that is what my mother once told me. All sorts of legacies such as deeds or money or jewelry were hidden in trunks and behind false walls and so on, and the person named in the will as the heir could inherit only if he or she could find where something had been hidden. But if the estate was entailed and there were no funds apart from that, what could he have hidden?"

Cousin Roberta shook her head pityingly. "No sense of history, any of you. Have you forgotten the China trade? Your grandfather was one of the first to really visit the Orient. He made himself quite useful to the Manchurian emperor at a difficult time for the fellow, and although the aid he gave could not be acknowledged publicly, the emperor expressed his gratitude with an extremely valuable gift."

The viscount considered his cousin, trying to

decide how best to phrase himself. Before he could frame a suitable reply, his sister had spoken for him. "But, Cousin Roberta," Nella said, her eyes wide with interest, "*what* gift? Didn't Grandfather ever show it to you?"

"Particularly as you have said you were his favorite," Stanwood could not resist pointing out.

With something of a sniff, Cousin Roberta pulled her shawl tighter about her shoulders. "He said it was too precious and was afraid to bring it out where the servants or someone might see it," she explained plaintively. "Said that since he'd found a good place to hide it, he wasn't about to be a fool and give the game away."

At this point Theodosia said quietly, "So you have never actually seen proof that there was such a treasure?"

"Well, no . . ." Cousin Roberta said reluctantly.

"And it seems strange he entrusted such a message to you, when he could not have been sure that you would outlive his son," Theodosia went on thoughtfully.

"But he was certain!" Miss Stanwood retorted tearfully. "Said he always knew his son would stick his spoon in the wall at an early age because of the reckless way he went about everything! And everyone knows the women in the Stanwood family have always lived much longer than the men. Much longer. Isn't that so, Bartram?"

"Of course it is," he replied soothingly. "And even if it were not, I expect he knew you would leave a letter behind or some such thing."

Roberta's eyes glittered strangely as she said, "Oh, that's what he thought, right enough. I just never got around to writing the wretched thing, is all. And now there is no need."

"But—" Theodosia started to protest.

Indignantly Nella rounded on her friend. "How can you doubt Cousin Roberta's story, Dosie?" she demanded. "Or want to? Why . . . why, it would be beyond anything great if *we* were to discover the treasure! If it takes the last bit of summer and all of the fall, we must do it!"

Over Helena's head Theodosia and the viscount found that their eyes met and that they shared the same thought. Neither was about to disparage an activity that might keep the girl out of trouble. Indeed, the viscount went so far as to reply soothingly, "*I* certainly have no objection if you and Lady Theodosia choose to search for such a treasure. I merely beg that the pair of you acquit me of any need to join you."

Scornfully Helena snorted, "You needn't fear, Bartram, *we* shan't plague you for your company. You shall be able to ignore us entirely."

"I wish that were true," he retorted dryly. Then, glancing at his watch, he said, "Enough. We'd best all seek our beds now, for I intend a very early start in the morning."

Amid the protests and amiable jesting that followed, no one noticed the gleam of satisfaction in Cousin Roberta's eyes. But then, scarcely anyone ever noticed Cousin Roberta at all.

5

Miss Clarissa Cranley stood on the steps of the mansion at Stanwood Oaks. She never failed to delight in the scene that met her eyes, nor to recollect the land she could not see. A sweeping lawn was before her, and a drive that was lined with the oaks that gave the estate its name. Behind the mansion, she knew, were several hundred more acres and a lake, as well as an elegant garden. Inside the brick house were long corridors and a comfortable number of rooms, all furnished with the best that London could offer over the past twenty-five years as well as with family heirlooms, some of which were over three hundred years old. The house cried out for a mistress to take charge of it. Someone, Miss Cranley could not resist thinking, just like herself. *Not* that she had been requested to be present today. No, she had decided quite on her own to be useful. Miss Cranley could not resist being useful. Particularly to dear Bartram. The only difficulty was, did he appreciate it?

It was an important question. At two months short of twenty, with her one London Season long behind her, Miss Cranley had begun to despair of ever finding an acceptable suitor. Not that she was precisely an antidote; quite the opposite in fact. Her eyes were fine and the features of her face regular enough to satisfy the most exacting critic. Her figure was nicely trim and her height just right, one admirer had told her, to rest against a gentleman's shoulders. If her clothes were not of the first stare, it might have been argued that that showed a pleasantly serious turn of mind that placed other matters above mere fashion. In short, upon appearance it would have seemed that Miss Cranley should have had no shortage of suitors. But she did. Never one to have made a great many childhood friends, she still had had her share of admirers. The trouble was, however, that they never seemed to last. Until the Viscount Stanwood. As a boy he had disliked her intensely, thinking her far too prissy, but in the past six months he had seemed to alter his opinion. Indeed, more than one motherly woman in the area had commented to Miss Cranley on how particular the viscount's attentions had become. And yet he had rushed off to Bath just as she had thought he was about to throw her the handkerchief. Miss Cranley was not in the least certain she could take her position for granted.

Another young woman might have told

Stanwood that she had been riding by and stopped to speak to the housekeeper, whose daughter worked at *her* father's house, and that it was coincidence that dear Bartram had returned home the same day. Miss Cranley, however, was far too honest for that. The housekeeper had told her that the viscount had sent word he was returning with his sister and one of Helena's schoolgirl friends. Nothing more had been needed to convince Clarissa that Bartram would be glad of her support, and so she would say. Though Helena was only three years younger, Clarissa could not help but think of her as a child, and no doubt it would be the same with Helena's little friend. Bartram would never have the patience to be able to deal with them on his own! It was with utter complacence, therefore, that she watched the viscount's smart traveling coach round the bend to the drive and pull up in front of the house.

A moment later, however, Miss Clarissa Cranley suffered a severe shock. The first carriage halted some distance down the drive, the door opened, and two young women *tumbled* out in the most harum-scarum way! The next moment they were *running* toward the house and drawing up short only when they caught sight of her. The shock was not at their behavior, for it was only what Miss Cranley would have expected of Bartram's young sister. The child had been in one scrape or another for her heedlessness ever since Clarissa could remember. No, the shock came at the sight of Helena's friend. This was no child, and instinctively Clarissa felt the unknown young woman was going to mean trouble for her. A shiver ran through Miss Cranley as she found herself wondering just why dear Bartram had invited the young woman to visit Stanwood Oaks.

To be sure, Bartram followed directly, dismounting from his horse, and greeting her in the most amiable way, but he made no effort to chastise either girl save to say mildly, "You might introduce Miss Cranley, Nella."

At that moment Clarissa Cranley felt a strong surge of anger. Breeding took over, however, and she advanced to greet the young ladies, a cool smile firmly fixed upon her face.

"What are *you* doing here, Issy?" Helena demanded petulantly. But before Miss Cranley could answer, she went on with her usual carelessness, "Have you ever met Dosie? Of course not. Dosie, this is Issy. A neighbor."

With a frosty smile Clarissa took the hand held out to her. "I am Miss Clarissa Cranley," she said formally.

"And I am Lady Theodosia Elston," came the equally formal reply.

"I should have guessed it from your behavior just now." She paused and added condescendingly, "Even here we have heard of your family. They are all, one gathers, quite lively."

As Nella gasped in anger behind her, Theodosia responded tranquilly, "Indeed? But then, of course, we have none of us ever heard of you or your family. Minor country gentry, are they?"

At this point the viscount tried to intervene.

He was too late, however, and he began to realize that his temper was not improved by having Miss Cranley upon the scene, for Clarissa did have a way of setting up Nella's back.

His worst fears were realized as Clarissa turned away from Theodosia and said, "One must trust the servants did not witness your outrageousness just now, Nella. It would never do for it to get about the countryside that you are as much a hoyden as ever. Bartram was right to bring you home. You need someone to take you in hand, as your chaperon evidently could not do so. And now, shall we all go inside? I told Mrs. Thompson to start the tea the moment your carriage was in sight."

"Indeed?" Nella said innocently. "I didn't know you had become mistress of this house. Did Bartram sell it to you?"

Theodosia diverted the fire by turning and saying in her well-bred voice, "Don't you think, Nella, that we ought to see that your cousin Roberta has arrived safely, first?"

Helena's eyes glittered as she, too, turned her back on Clarissa and said sweetly, "Oh, yes, of course. Let us go help her out of her coach."

As they walked toward the carriage just now drawing up behind the viscount's, Theodosia said in a whisper to Helena, "I swear I can almost hear her gnashing her teeth. Who *is* Miss Clarissa Cranley?"

"Issy? Or 'Miss Prissy,' as we called her when we were children? I'm not certain, but Cousin Roberta has dropped a hint or two that Bartram was thinking of marriage. I only pray it may not be her. That would be doing it much too brown!" Helena wailed softly.

There was no time to speak further, however, for Cousin Roberta was stepping down from the coach. That redoubtable woman looked about her with satisfaction at the lawn and brick house. "Hasn't changed a bit since I was here last. Or since I was a girl," she said grimly. "Not on the outside, anyway. It's just the way it ought to be."

She paused and peered nearsightedly at the girls, who stood watching her. Hastily Helena said, "How was your ride? Would you like some tea? Miss Cranley said Mrs. Thompson would have it ready soon."

Once more Cousin Roberta was all meekness. "How thoughtful. Yes, tea sounds like just the thing. Come along, girls, I must greet this Miss Cranley, whoever she may be." She paused then and seemed to steel herself to speak. With a severity that lacked any real force behind it she said, "You know, Helena, Lady Theodosia, it really is not the thing to run like that across the green. Whatever possessed you to do it?"

Nella bent her head. "I'm sorry, Cousin Roberta. I was just so happy to be home, and I wanted Dosie's first sight of the house to be on foot. Her first close-up sight of it, I mean."

"Nevertheless, you are not to do it again!"

"Yes, Cousin Roberta."

Helena would not have been either surprised or pleased to learn that Clarissa Cranley and her brother were discussing precisely the same matter. The two of them had already entered the house and gone into the drawing room by the time the three other ladies reached the steps of the house, a circumstance Clarissa was grateful for.

"We haven't much time," she told Stanwood bluntly. "But I do wish to ask if you are angry at me for coming here today. I only meant, you see, to be helpful."

Stanwood took Miss Cranley's hand in his, a wry smile flitting across his face. "Angry with you?" he asked. "Impossible! You have been far too kind as well as helpful to me in this past year for me to take umbrage at anything you might do."

"Your sister has," Clarissa pointed out, gazing at the floor.

"My sister is a foolish young chit," Stanwood told her roundly. "One reason I wished to bring her here is that I hoped you might help me to curb her impulsiveness. I can only guess that she has been in one scrape or another ever since my father left her in his cousin Roberta's care."

"She did not take kindly to my words outside," Clarissa said with a sigh. "I am afraid I set up her back, and yet I only wished to do what was best for her, since someone must bring her to a realization of how her behavior must have appeared!"

Stanwood nodded reassuringly, his own irritation at Clarissa forgotten the moment they had crossed the threshold of Stanwood Oaks. "My sister is, as I said before, young and heedless.

I've no doubt, however, that as she comes to know you better your evident good sense will convince her to listen to you. That and a strong hand on my part!''

Miss Clarissa Cranley looked up at the viscount with such soft-eyed approval that had the three ladies not entered the room just then, he might have so far forgotten himself as to do far more than merely hold her hand.

6

The mansion at Stanwood Oaks had been built around 1700 by the current viscount's great-great-grandfather. To be sure, it had been built on the ruins of a far older house, but the last traces of that dwelling were now completely obliterated. The viscount had been a farsighted man and had had his home designed by the most advanced architects of his day. The mansion therefore boasted conveniences that few houses of its era could claim. With three floors and thirty-odd rooms it was also quite impressive. Built of red brick, it mixed the most delightful touches of the Queen Anne era with forerunners of the Georgian era, such as a fanlight over the door and simple rectangular windows. Later, wrought ironwork had been added, and plaster ceilings with elaborate paintings that dominated the main rooms.

Other features had been added by the viscounts that followed, and the mansion was one of the snuggest to be found outside of London, with chimneys that all drew without smoking, corridors that were remarkably free of drafts, and furnishings that would have put a London matron to shame. Indeed, the current viscount found himself thinking more and more that it was perhaps fortunate his father had invested so much money in renovations. The funds would otherwise only have gone for gambling or some other useless pursuit, whereas this way if it became necessary he could sell the place and realize an income sufficient to provide for himself and his sister. If only his father had shown such prudence elsewhere in his life.

Theodosia was aware of none of this. To her, the Oaks was merely an attractive house, larger and somewhat more comfortable than most, with perhaps less of a mixture of styles than was likely to be found in an older structure. Indeed, as Helena took her friend on a tour of the place, Theodosia found herself nodding approvingly at any number of handsome touches. There were even, to her astonishment, porcelain stoves in most of the upstairs sitting rooms used by the family, and she had little doubt that in winter these rooms would be enviously warm compared to those heated by a mere fireplace.

"Yes, but that doesn't matter right now," Helena said in exasperation as Theodosia asked where the stoves had come from. "We're supposed to be looking for Grandfather's papers! I'm only showing you these rooms so that if any of the servants ask what we're about, we can say I'm giving you a tour of the house."

Theodosia frowned thoughtfully. "You know, Nella, we've already looked in the rooms that were your grandfather's and then your father's—except for your brother's bedchamber, and that would be going a bit too far—and have found nothing. Perhaps his papers are in amongst your mother's."

Helena shook her head decisively. "Mama never had any papers. She rarely wrote letters, and the ones she received, she invariably tossed away after reading. Except for Papa's, of course. But anything else would have stood right out, and she would have turned them over to Papa straightaway. Besides, if they had discovered the inheritance, we should not be in the straits we are now."

Theodosia nodded doubtfully. "Where should we look, then?" she asked. "The library?"

Helena grimaced at her friend. "We shall find only books there. Books and Bartram's papers. Papa was used to say that all accounts and such belonged in the hands of his bailiff. I still don't see why Bartram dismissed the fellow. But in any event, if we found nothing in the upstairs book-room, a room Grandfather was supposed to have disdained, why should we find anything in the library?"

"In among the books, perhaps? We didn't consider that," Theodosia pointed out.

"Perhaps. But I should rather try elsewhere

first. And certainly I should wait until Bartram has gone out riding or to visit Miss Cranley or such. We don't want *him* interfering or claiming the credit, do we?"

"Of course not," Theodosia seconded her friend stoutly. "Well, then, where *do* we try next? We've been belowstairs in the kitchens and storerooms, and frankly, I can't believe anything hidden there. Nor in the main rooms. The attics, perhaps?"

Helena thought for a moment. "Yes," she agreed slowly, "for I don't believe we ought to invade the servants' quarters. They wouldn't like it, and I see no need. And as Grandfather was said rarely to leave the house, we may except the outbuildings as well, I should think. As you say, the attics would be our best course, at this point."

Theodosia looked down at her gown, the plainest she had brought, and said, "Well, at least we are dressed for it. I did foresee, you know, the possibility that we should find ourselves in such a circumstance. Lead the way, my dear."

At the far end of the third floor was the door to a narrow wooden stairway that led upward. From the thickness of the dust and plentiful presence of cobwebs, it seemed evident to the two young women that no one had been this way in some time. Fortunately, Helena had had the presence of mind to bring along a small lamp and Theodosia held a candelabrum with lighted tapers. Once they reached the top of the stairs, however, matters were much improved. Narrow windows allowed in sufficient light so that the candles and lamp were scarcely needed.

As the two young women looked about them at the boxes and bundles and furniture and knick-knacks that had found their way up to the attic, Theodosia said bluntly, "I hope you have some notion of where to begin, Nella, for otherwise we shall be here for days!"

Helena looked about thoughtfully. "Some of the boxes and things I recall as my mother's or father's. And some are surely too old to be what we seek. Here, this lot over here—let's try these first."

The trunks yielded little beyond dresses and petticoats and laces and furbelows popular some fifty years before. "My grandmother's things," Helena noted succinctly.

"And these are your grandfather's," Theodosia replied, holding up a waistcoat and rummaging among buckles and stockings and even a pair of shoes. "But no papers or books or such, I'm afraid."

"Well, keep looking, there ought to be something up here!" Helena retorted impatiently.

It was Theodosia who finally spotted the worn sea chest half-hidden in a corner behind the larger trunks. Had it ever held a lock, it was long since broken, and she was able to open the lid easily. "Nella," she said in a queer voice, "come over and look at this."

"What is it? What have you found?" her friend demanded, crowding in to see.

In answer Theodosia held out a scrap of richly

embroidered silk and a pair of matching house shoes. Immediately Helena snatched the fabric, fingering it gently. "I remember this," she said in a thoughtful tone. "Papa had some old robe of his father's cut up to make a waistcoat for himself and some pillows for Mama's drawing rooms. He said there had once been much more of the fabric but that Grandfather wouldn't tell him where to find it. Now I see that it must have come from China. What else is in there?"

Hastily Theodosia turned back to the sea chest and rummaged through it again. After a moment she turned to her friend, a distinct look of triumph in her eyes. In her hands she held a bound volume that looked almost as faded as the chest. "A journal or diary?" she suggested even before she had opened it to see.

Together Theodosia and Helena held the dusty volume. At randon Helena began to read fragments aloud:

> Crossed the channel with free traders. Banished after Culloden. Stuart has lost. No time to retrieve anything from home.
>
> Must leave France. Funds running low, opportunities to be had from Marseilles. Perhaps with pirates.
>
> Plumper in the pocket. Heading farther east.
>
> Landed at Castle Zelandia, Dutch trading post on coast of China.
>
> Have reached imperial court. Received as scholar, but with suspicion.
>
> Rapid progress with language. Do not admit to

same. Am gathering much useful information this way.

Received today by emperor. No one is allowed to speak his name. He is known by his *nein hao* or title, as Ch'ien Lung.

Uprising in west. Am being sent as messenger. Opportunities here.

Emperor is pleased with me. Have been introduced to generals Chao-hui and A-kuei. Further trouble brewing.

Much traveling, delivering of dispatches.

Emperor extremely pleased.

Trouble brewing at court. Time to leave for coast while am still in favor.

Sailing tomorrow for Canton.

Helena looked up from the book she held. "It ends there," she said quietly. "Though there's much more in between, of course. I think we'd best take it downstairs, where I can read it better. But at least there can be no doubt my grandfather *was* in China."

"No doubt at all," Theodosia replied dryly. "He seems to have been a very resourceful fellow. Now, where did we leave the candles and the lamp? It must be almost time for tea."

When they arrived downstairs, it was to discover that Miss Clarissa Cranley was waiting in the drawing room. With something that sounded very much like a curse to Theodosia, Helena said, "You go in, Dosie, and greet her. I shall run upstairs to my room and hide the journal."

With a final warning look, Helena met Theodosia's eyes and then started up the stairs. Behind her Theodosia turned right and, a moment later, opened the door of the drawing room to see Miss Cranley framed by the linen curtains of one of the windows, staring out at the fine lawn.

Miss Roberta Stanwood was seated at a small table preparing to pour out tea for her guest. Theodosia greeted both of them. Clarissa professed to be all delight. "Lady Theodosia! How nice to see you again. Are you enjoying your stay?" Her eyes narrowed as she took in Theodosia's appearance, and she said, "Whatever have you been doing? Sweeping out the attics?"

Theodosia looked down at her dress. A drab brown color and never particularly fashionable, it was now covered with cobwebs and dirt. "Oh, dear," she said, "Nella did take me on a rather thorough tour of the house. I'd best go upstairs and change."

In spite of herself, Miss Cranley wrinkled her nose slightly as she said, "Yes, yes, I do think that would be wise. Not that I wish to criticize, my dear, but such disarray really does not belong in a drawing room."

When she came back downstairs a short quarter of an hour later, it was to find that Miss Cranley was preparing to take her leave. "But what is this?" Theodosia protested. "I did not think I was that long in changing my things."

Miss Cranley forced herself to smile. "You were

not," she said curtly. "I find it difficult, however, to stay in a place where I am not wanted."

As she took a seat, Theodosia instinctively looked to the viscount, who stood on the far side of the room regarding the fireplace fixedly. Then she looked at Helena's crimson face. "Now that is an absolute bouncer!" Nella retorted hotly. "Merely because I said you had no right to tell me how to conduct myself, *you* have taken snuff."

Defensively Clarissa replied, the smile still firmly fixed about her lips, "I merely thought to give you a hint, my dear. Placed without a mother, as you are, someone must do so. I am persuaded you can only be the better for someone to tell you that such Bath manners will not do here in the country. That it is not the thing to go out riding alone. Or . . . or running across the lawns as you did the day you arrived. I say nothing about Lady Theodosia's behavior, for she is not Bartram's sister and therefore it is not my part to criticize. But you both ought to know that excessiveness in dress will not be marked with approval here, either."

"What you mean is," Nella shot back before Dosie could stop her, "is that you are envious because your clothes are so dowdy and you cannot be honest enough to admit it!"

"Envy you?" Clarissa permitted herself a short, incredulous laugh. "Fashion must always envy propriety, scarcely the other way around."

"Quite right," Cousin Roberta put in from her

corner, where everyone had forgotten her presence.

"Do you not agree also?" Miss Cranley asked Theodosia sweetly.

Theodosia paused and looked about her. Helena had changed to a delightful dress of green muslin that was, nevertheless, more than a year old and a trifle small on her. Stanwood might have decreed that the year of mourning was sufficiently close to an end that Helena might return to colors, but there had not yet been any funds forthcoming to replace the dresses she had all but outgrown. As for Miss Roberta Stanwood, she was dressed in her inevitable black dress that might have been designed at any time in the past twenty years. Stanwood was dressed impeccably in dark breeches and coat, but they, too, had the air of having been much worn. Only Theodosia herself was dressed with any hint of fashion. Her dress of blue muslin was far newer than Helena's and had come from London. This sally, then, was directed at her.

Theodosia looked down at her hands, which were folded neatly in her lap, then fixed her gaze on Clarissa's dress of some lavender cloth chosen more for its serviceability than out of any consideration of fashion. Demurely she said, "Why, yes, I agree that fashion without propriety is to be deprecated, particularly in the country, where no one will appreciate it. But I also find that propriety without fashion is needlessly hard on the eyes that must gaze upon it."

The gasp of hastily suppressed laughter came not, as Theodosia had expected, from Helena but rather from her brother. Miss Cranley turned outraged eyes upon Stanwood, who was helpless to keep the amusement out of his eyes. With a somewhat quivering lip he told her, "Lady Theodosia has you there, I am afraid."

But Miss Cranley was made of stern stuff and she replied, a sweet edge to her now soft voice, "I had thought that you, at least, would understand, Stanwood. You have told me more than once that your mother's extravagance in clothes and trinkets and such helped to bring the estate to its current low level."

The darkness returned to the viscount's face and he did not contradict her. Helena started to protest, and he cut her short. "You know nothing of the accounts, Nella. I have had to deal with little else for the past year."

"It is not important," Miss Cranley said with a tight smile. "In any event, I had come particularly to invite you and your sister and her friend to a dinner party we are having in three days' time. I know it is short notice, but in the country we do not stand upon ceremony. So if you will take potluck with us, I do not think you will be disappointed."

"Of course we shall come," Stanwood said immediately. "It is very kind of you to invite us."

Miss Cranley's smile was a bit wider as she replied, "I had thought it would be a kindness to give Helena the chance to go about a bit among country folk before she must make her curtsy to the *ton* in London. She will not wish to go there entirely lacking in social skills."

Before Helena could answer, Stanwood hastily offered to walk Miss Cranley to her carriage. Graciously she accepted and with her head held high led the way out of the room. Behind them Helena and Theodosia watched silently. Cousin Roberta, on the other hand, began to chatter. "A most estimable young lady. I do hope your brother asks for her hand. So romantic, don't you think? And how nice of her to invite you to dinner. Not everyone would be so thoughtful."

"Nice?" Helena snorted. "More than likely Issy merely wanted to have Dosie come so that she could tell all the neighbors that she is on the most familiar terms with the daughter of an earl! You know she has always had a weakness for titles and such."

"I know no such thing," Miss Roberta Stanwood said severely, "nor should you, even if it were true, which I am persuaded it is not. Surely, as the young woman your brother may wed, Miss Cranley is merely trying to do you a good turn. She is quite right, Helena, that it will not do for you to arrive in London a green girl ignorant of all society."

"And what, pray tell me, Cousin Roberta, was it I did in Bath if not mingle a trifle in society?" Helena demanded indignantly.

"You know very well that was only in the most informal way," Roberta told her sharply.

"And so this is to be," Helena answered. "That's what Issy said."

"She is Miss Cranley, and so you are to address her," Miss Stanwood told her charge.

Hastily Theodosia intervened, well aware of the look of rebellion fixed upon Helena's face. "Whatever the cause for Miss Cranley's invitation," she said firmly, "we must be grateful, Nella. I can imagine nothing more tedious than forever to be seeing only our own faces over the dinner table every day. Surely even an evening at the Cranley household is to be preferred to that?" Helena merely continued to gaze stubbornly at Theodosia, who went on coaxingly, "Come, come, Nella, where is your sense of humor? Surely it is at least as difficult for Miss Cranley to entertain two young ladies she dislikes as much as she dislikes us as it is for us to be there. Let us go and be on our best behavior and put her to the test of her patience. And perhaps we shall find she has invited other guests, whom we may even enjoy speaking to!"

"Quite right, Lady Theodosia," Stanwood said, entering the room just in time to hear the last of her words. "I have it upon excellent authority the Cranleys will make every effort to see that you and my sister enjoy the evening. I wish, Nella, that you could be as full of charity toward Clarissa as Lady Theodosia. She has only the kindest wishes for you and is merely trying to guide you in a way I cannot. It is, I know, one of her fondest wishes to stand as, if not a mother, then a guiding hand to you."

There could be no answer to that, and both girls were grateful that Stanwood allowed them to turn the talk to other matters.

7

Sir Thomas Holwell was the sort of gentleman that most mothers would have given a great deal to have as a son-in-law. He was courteous, well-dressed, impeccably pedigreed, and possessor of a quite handsome inheritance. He was neither a man-milliner nor a blood of the sports fields. If he was inclined to sample deeply a host's wine stock, nevertheless, no one had ever seen him the worse for wear, nor had he a reputation as one who was fond of blue ruin or low company. His inheritance was untouched by the losses of excess gambling, and yet the fellow was always welcome when another hand was needed at cards. No breath of scandal had ever linked Sir Thomas with any lady or any member of the *demimonde*. This argued either an exquisite discretion or a disinterest in the sex, belied by his constant willingness to partner ladies at a dance or escort them to the theatre or other entertainments. No hostess could have ever asked for a more charming guest nor one who would need less guidance in the drawing out of shier young ladies.

In short, Sir Thomas Holwell was something of a paragon and yet had, at the age of one-and-thirty, somehow escaped the bonds of marriage. Not that he was above being pleased by each year's new crop of beauties; indeed he had a kind word for each one of them. And that was the problem. He was pleased but never quite pleased enough. Though the family title might be a modest one, he could not help but feel that duty required him to choose a lady both lovely and unusual and from as illustrious a family as his own. So he looked on with a smile and a willingness to be pleased, but it was not until he met the Lady Theodosia Elston that Sir Thomas felt all his criteria had been met.

Blessed with perfect patience, however, and a desire to be certain, Sir Thomas pursued his courtship discreetly. He would not be the one to try to tempt Lady Theodosia to stand up for more than two dances at a ball, nor single her out for intimate conversation. Indeed it was only when he followed her to Bath after she was so hastily returned there that Theodosia had become certain of his interest in her. As it was, Sir Thomas never called more than twice a week, nor stayed longer than the prescribed time for a morning visit. And if business required him to leave Bath for short periods of time, he went without the slightest hint of disappointment at parting from Theodosia.

Such a separation had come about a few days before the Viscount Stanwood arrived in Bath and decided to remove his sister from her dangerous situation there. So rapidly did Stanwood act that they were gone before Sir Thomas had returned from London, and so he had no notion that Lady Theodosia had even contemplated a retreat from Bath until he arrived at her grandmother's house to invite both ladies to go for a short stroll. *Then* he discovered she was gone to the south and east for an unknown period of time! Lady Willoughby was all kind attention, but there was, it seemed, very little she could tell him.

"Well, *where* is she, Lady Willoughby? Can you at least tell me that much?" he finally demanded in exasperation.

Lady Willoughby spread her hands helplessly. "I told you: she has gone to stay with a friend in the country. With Helena Stanwood."

"Yes, but where?"

"Stanwood Acres, Stanwood Oaks, something like that. And don't ask me for precise directions, for I don't really know where it is. Look it up in the list of peerages if you must know. That is what I should have done if I needed to reach her."

Holwell looked at Lady Willoughby in disbelief. A trifle icily he said, "I wonder that, as her chaperon, you did not feel it necessary to go along as well."

Lady Willoughby shrugged placidly. "I did think of it, you know, but my health would not stand for such a journey. Besides, Miss Stan-wood's chaperon will be there, and I am certain the viscount is a perfect gentleman."

"The viscount will be there?" Holwell de-manded. Abruptly a new train of thought occurred to him, and he asked harshly, "How long has she been acquainted with Stanwood?"

Lady Willoughby continued to smile placidly at her guest. A hint of impishness lit her eyes, how-ever, as she replied, "Why, long enough, I sup-pose, for the viscount to satisfy himself as to Theodosia's character."

This time Holwell could not contain his anger. "I trust," he said, "that you have not traded your granddaughter's happiness for a title and an empty estate. In the event you did not already know it, I take leave to tell you Stanwood's coffers are empty."

"I did know it," Lady Willoughby replied, a hint of steel in her voice, "and I take leave to tell *you* that your manners are abominable. In any event, what is done is done, and you can do nothing to alter it."

"I wonder you are so calm," he said, "but I can assure you that I am not." Biting off his words, Holwell added, "As for whether I can do anything to alter the matter, well, we shall see. Good day, Lady Willoughby."

Placidly Lady Willoughby watched him leave. When he was gone, a look of utter satisfaction filled her face. This shall, she told herself happily, bring that idiot up to scratch. Now it is Dosie's job to have the sense to accept him. Unless, that is, she had managed to bring round the viscount. In spite of his Friday face, I did rather like him better. Indeed, it all makes me think of when I was a young widow, just thirty-seven and still the Countess of Elston.

Lady Willoughby's thoughts drifted back to that time when the entire Elston family and her own had been scandalized because she chose to remarry no more than a year after the earl's death, and to a mere baron, as Theodosia had called him. Well, so he had been. Lord Willoughby, a handsome fellow of forty-five years and a widower, had come calling upon the young widow in London and fallen in love with her. That he had a title and was as plump in the pocket as any Elston mattered not a jot to either the countess or her family. Blithely she wed him and angrily the family had refused to accept the news. No longer Lady Constance, Countess of Elston, she became merely Lady Willoughby. Eventually, of course, the family mellowed and would have given her once more the courtesy of calling her by the finer title, but Lady Willoughby would have none of it. Lady Willoughby she had become and Lady Willoughby she would remain, for she was quite content to be a mere baroness.

Lady Willoughby sighed. Those had been good years, the twenty she had spent with his lordship. She had been fond of the earl, her first husband, but it had not been a love match. Though they dealt well together, there had never been the earnest need for one another that Constance had felt with Lord Willoughby. Nor was it a contradiction that after his death Constance had grieved, then looked about her for another husband. For Lord Willoughby had been as kind on his death-bed as he had in health, and he had given her firm orders not to dwindle into lonely widowhood. She was to take the first good chance at happy companionship she saw, and damn what any relatives might say!

But Lady Willoughby had never found another man she wished to marry, and so, eleven years later she was still Lady Willoughby and content to have it so. Now her matchmaking schemes were all centered upon her granddaughter Theodosia, and even that looked to resolve itself soon.

With a silent laugh to herself at the notion of Holwell and Stanwood coming face to face with one another, Lady Willoughby thought: Well, now Dosie won't be bored. Makes me almost wish I had chosen to go with her. Then I wouldn't have missed the fun. But I would have missed Amanda's card party and Caroline's supper and . . .

Sir Thomas Holwell neither knew nor cared about the card parties or suppers or other social engagements that held Lady Willoughby in Bath. He had been shocked to his core to discover that she had allowed the Lady Theodosia to travel alone to the country estate of Viscount Stanwood. That Miss Helena Stanwood was bringing *her* chaperon along mattered not a jot. Lady Theodosia ought to have someone along to look after her. True, Sir Thomas could not say that he had heard anything to name Stanwood as an unscrupulous fellow; nevertheless, the need to fill empty family coffers might well tempt the gentleman to pressure a helpless young lady to marry him. And Lady Theodosia was young. That was precisely one of the things Sir Thomas liked about her. She needed taking care of.

It was therefore with a strong sense of urgency that Sir Thomas ordered a stunned valet to repack his bags and pay the shot at the inn for they were about to leave at once on the southern road. Without waiting for a reply, Holwell hurried out to have his carriage brought round, and within the hour they were on their way. He was *not* going to abandon Lady Theodosia to the viscount!

Had Miss Cranley known of Sir Thomas Holwell's intentions, she would no doubt have approved heartily. As it was, she was casting about in vain for the names of eligible young gentlemen to invite to her potluck dinner. Of course her brother would be there, but one could not count upon him to please Bartram's guest. Indeed, he would certainly not have pleased Clarissa. Unfortunately, most of the eligible young gentlemen had left the surrounding countryside for more interesting places. The ones that were left were those rusticating for some social offense committed against the *ton* or hiding out from creditors or those with insufficient credit to visit London in the first place. One simply could not invite them to dine with

Lady Theodosia Elston. And yet it was imperative that Clarissa find *someone* to invite. Already
Clarissa found herself uneasy at the amount of
time Bartram appeared to spend in the girl's
company, and she felt that all would be right only
if she could hit upon someone to distract the girl.

8

Stanwood stood and looked around him, not really seeing the rows and rows of books that lined the walls of the library, nor even the tables and other wooden objects made from the trees of the estate. Instead he strode past an armchair and lifted aside one of the blue velvet curtains to look outside. The view was of the back of the house, and one could catch a glimpse of the corner of the stables. The place where Stanwood had no doubt his sister and her friend would soon be. He could not help being aware that it was their custom to go out riding every morning, and he only hoped it would keep them out of mischief. With Clarissa's warning in mind, he decided to join them.

When he reached the stables a short time later, one of the grooms was helping Nella and her friend mount two of the liveliest mares in the Stanwood stables. Bartram raised his eyebrows but said nothing. If Lady Theodosia was as fine a horsewoman as his sister, he had nothing to worry about. And indeed she seemed to have an air of decided competence about her as she neatly brought the restless mare under control. The grim lines about the viscount's mouth softened as he watched her, a trim figure in a riding habit of vivid green that was far more fashionable than the slightly faded blue one his sister wore. I am very fortunate, he thought, that Nella has a friend here to keep her company. Otherwise—

Nella's voice slashed across the viscount's thoughts as she cried out sharply, "Bartram! What are you doing here?"

"Am I so cruel a brother that you must greet me with such suspicion?" he asked with a lightness belied by the shadows about his eyes. "If so, in this you are quite mistaken. I have been up since dawn, and felt the need of a good gallop. Something I felt sure you could promise me, Nella. In short, I mean to ride with you today."

Helena continued to watch her brother warily, and on impulse Theodosia smiled warmly at him. Indeed, it was scarcely a sacrifice, for he appeared quite handsome in his riding clothes. It was, she realized with something of a shock, the first time she had seen Stanwood dressed other than in black. She could not know, but did guess, that the expense of outfitting himself with mourning clothes suitable for country riding had been one he had chosen to spare the already beleaguered estate. The wind ruffling his hair only made Stanwood seem somehow more vulnerable, and she found herself wishing she could reach out and stroke away the lines that creased his brow. Instead she said aloud, "You are kind to take the time away from your work. It cannot be other than a dead bore for you to entertain us."

So friendly was Theodosia's voice that Bartram actually found himself smiling at her. As he swung up onto the horse the groom had just brought out, he said, "A bore? Not at all. I should far rather be out riding than inside with the dusty accounts. Indeed, I almost feel as if I were playing hooky."

"Something I feel sure you rarely do," Theodosia retorted dryly.

"Except to visit Clarissa," Helena chimed in, "which he certainly does often enough!" Then, looking away and briskly surveying the horizon, she said, "Which way do we go today?"

Without hesitation, Bartram pointed. "Toward the coast."

"To the ruins?" Helena asked in a voice that was half-awe, half-excitement.

"To the ruins," the viscount said.

"But Mama and Papa told us never to go there," his sister protested.

Bartram looked at her directly. "That was a good many years ago, when we were still children. And the reason was Jeremy's death. But we are no longer children, and in any case, we are none of us going there alone, but rather together. It will be quite safe, I assure you, Lady Theodosia."

Coolly Dosie met his eyes. "I am not afraid," she said frankly, and as if to prove it, started her horse off in the direction he had indicated.

In a moment Bartram's horse and Nella's were beside hers. "If I have offended you . . ." Bartram began awkwardly.

Theodosia smiled and shook her head. "You have not. But I am curious. Who was Jeremy?"

There was a long moment in which Theodosia was very much aware of the wind tugging at her riding bonnet. Then Nella's voice and the viscount's tumbled over one another.

"Our brother . . ."

"He was twelve and wandering among the ruins . . ."

"A rock slide began and he was trapped underneath . . ."

"One of the stable hands found him when his horse returned alone . . ."

"After three days in pain he died . . ."

Once again there was silence, and Theodosia broke it by asking, "How long ago was this?"

Helena let Bartram answer. "Ten years ago. So you can see why our parents forbade us to visit the ruins."

"How horrible for you," Theodosia replied gently. "But you go there now?"

He nodded. "Jeremy was a heedless lad and I suspect he was climbing where he ought not to have been and somehow triggered the rock slide himself, for there has never been once since. So it is perfectly safe for us." He paused as though searching for words, then went on, "In the past year I have found myself going there often, particularly when I have had to make difficult decisions about the estate. The ruins are, we believe, on the site of the first house built on Stanwood land."

"Destroyed by the Vikings," Nella added. "In fact we roast Bartram that he got his name from them, for it *is* a Viking name, you know."

At this the viscount shrugged irritably and said, "Nonsense. It is only a guess. For all we know, a distant ancestor simply could not spell Bertram. The only thing we know for certain is that it is an old family name."

"But the sea is not so far away," Helena persisted playfully. "Not more than three miles from here, and even less from the ruins." And before he could answer, she spurred her horse to a gallop and called out behind her, "Race you, Dosie!"

Something, however, held Theodosia back, and instead of watching Nella, she observed the lines deepening in disapproval about her host's mouth. Abruptly he became aware of her gaze and demanded curtly, "Well? What are you staring at? I should have thought you would be hard upon Nella's heels. Are you the Puritan you seemed to be the first time we met? Or are you simply afraid?"

At the contempt in his voice, Theodosia drew in her breath sharply, and for a moment matters hung in the balance. Then she let it out again and replied mildly, "Why, no, I am not quite a Puritan, but I confess I *was* curious to see if you would be. You seem to be displeased, but it is harmless, you know, and far better than other things she might set her mind upon. As for fear, well, I shall let you decide the matter!"

Theodosia concluded upon a definite note of challenge and urged her horse forward at the fastest pace it could accomplish. It took Stanwood scarcely a moment to recover, and then he, too, was racing. Ahead of him he could see Lady Theodosia turn her head back to look at him, tendrils of hair escaping from her bonnet. He drew even and then ahead, ignoring the cry of impatience that escaped her lips. Indeed he did not slacken until he reached his sister, who had already dismounted at the edge of the ruins. He did the same and was ready to assist Theodosia when she arrived moments later.

"Unfair!" she flung at him as he lifted her down from her horse.

"How so?" he asked, grinning easily.

Theodosia met his eyes squarely. "I don't know," she admitted crossly, "but it must have been, for I have never lost a race in my life."

"Well, you both lost to me!" Nella pointed out smugly. "I told you not to wear such a tightly fitted riding jacket, Dosie."

As the viscount's eyes rested on her speculatively, Theodosia felt herself color, and she turned away. A trifle breathlessly she said, "Are these the ruins, then? I should have thought a house that dated from the time of the Vikings would have been mostly wood, but there are so many stones here."

At her shoulder Stanwood's voice replied amiably, "This is the *site* of the first Stanwood dwelling, we believe, but there have been several in between."

"Our family has a positive talent for having the family homestead torn down about their heads," Helena added with relish. "Why we Stanwoods have never been able to keep out of political scrapes is far beyond me. Even that journal we found seems to indicate that grandfather was not above such things."

"Journal? What journal?" the viscount asked with a quick frown.

Theodosia calmly settled herself on a nearby stone to watch as Helena explained *this* trespass away.

Nella was having trouble meeting her brother's eyes. "Well," she said, twisting the fabric of her skirt, "Cousin Roberta did say there was some sort of inheritance, and Dosie and I agreed that if we were to look through Grandfather's old papers we might find some clue as to what and where it was."

"I see," Stanwood replied grimly. "And did you?"

"We did," Nella told him defiantly. "At least we found his journal, and let me tell you that was no easy matter, for it was *not* in the library where one might have expected to find something of such importance."

"Where did you find it?" Bartram asked uneasily.

"Up in one of the attic rooms in an old sea chest. It was Dosie's idea to check up there. Wasn't that clever of her?" Helena demanded eagerly.

With a quirk of his eyebrows at his houseguest,

Bartram replied dryly, "Very clever. And did you find what you were looking for in the journal?"

Helena bit her lower lip. "Not precisely. Although we did discover that Cousin Roberta was right. About Grandfather going to China, I mean. And we discovered why he was sent. It's so fascinating, Bartram. Why, he practically had to flee the country to save his life!"

"You are exaggerating!" Stanwood retorted sharply.

For the first time Theodosia spoke. "Actually she is not. Your ancestor appears to have become involved in the troubles with Scotland."

"*His* father could not afford to buy him a post in the government, having lost a great deal of money in the South Sea Bubble affair, and Grandfather thought he might gain a post with Stuart if *he* won the throne, I expect," Nella added helpfully.

Bartram frowned at his sister, and Theodosia once more took up the tale. "When it was discovered that your grandfather had been with the Stuart supporters at Culloden, he was under interdict and your family hastily shipped him out of the country. He had, I believe, the notion of becoming a pirate," she concluded innocently.

"A pirate?" the viscount exploded in exasperation. "You have far too vivid an imagination, both of you. I think I had best see this journal for myself and sort out this farrago of nonsense you have been roasting me with. I am sorry, Lady Theodosia, but a tour of these ruins shall have to wait for another day. Well? Come along."

Theodosia and Helena looked at one another and then shrugged. Why not? Watching Bartram read the journal promised to be far more amusing anyway.

9

For whatever reason, the three decided to ride around to the front of the house. As they did, the viscount exclaimed in surprise, "Who the devil is visiting me now?"

Amused, Theodosia roasted him, "I begin to think visitors arrive almost constantly here. And you said this was such a quiet place!"

"Alas, a curse of the family!" Helena chimed in with a melodramatic roll of her eyes before she began to giggle.

"Silence, you little peagoose," her brother told her sternly. "You don't want whoever it is to hear you."

Helena was about to retort in kind when Theodosia forestalled her. "I can scarcely credit it," she said, stunned. "Holwell!"

By now all three could see the tall figure of a gentleman in earnest conversation with Stanwood's servants. "You know the fellow?" Bartram asked Theodosia with surprise.

"Of course," Helena answered gleefully. "He's her fiancé!"

"*Nella!*" Theodosia protested.

"Well, he aspires to be her fiancé," Helena amended with an unabashed grin.

With an unexpected grimness Stanwood asked, "Is this true?"

Under the fierceness of his gaze, Theodosia lowered hers. "I . . . I suppose so," she answered with unusual hesitancy. "But I swear I had no notion he would follow me here!"

"But now that he is here, we must ask him to stay," Helena said breathlessly. "Just think, Bartram, we may witness their bethrothal!"

"No, there is no need—" Theodosia began to protest.

The viscount cut her short. "There is every need," he said curtly. "I presume Holwell is acceptable to your family. Or is this," Stanwood amended with sudden suspicion, "a clandestine affair?"

"Scarcely," Theodosia said with emphasis. "Nothing would more delight my grandmother than to hear that Sir Thomas has come up to scratch and that I have accepted him. Even Mama would no doubt be relieved. Her greatest fear, you know, is that she shall return to England someday and find her daughter still unwed and in need of a chaperon. *Not* a role my mama plays well."

With impeccable politeness and without the least trace of emotion Stanwood said, "In that case we must most certainly welcome Sir Thomas as our guest. He shall stay as long as he wishes."

And without waiting for Theodosia's reply, the viscount spurred his horse ahead and dismounted at the foot of the steps to his home. From where they followed, Theodosia and Helena could hear him say, "Sir Thomas? Welcome to Stanwood Oaks."

Abruptly Theodosia turned her horse and rode in the opposite direction, around back to the stables. With a gurgle of laughter, Helena followed. Behind them the two gentlemen regarded the exit of the ladies with tolerant amusement.

"No doubt Lady Theodosia wished to make herself more presentable," Sir Thomas said with approval. "She has a proper distaste for being in the least bit disarrayed or dusty."

"Quite so," Stanwood replied politely.

Recollecting abruptly that it was Stanwood who had lured Lady Theodosia to this rural setting, Holwell adopted a somewhat more austere tone. "I realize, Stanwood, that you must think it rather rude of me to appear here without invitation, but I must tell you that I believe Lady Theodosia's welfare to be some concern of mine."

The viscount held up a hand and said amiably, "Please. No apologies are necessary, I assure you. You are quite welcome to stay with us as long as you like."

Holwell stared at Stanwood in disbelief. "Well, well, that is kind of you," he said. "My bags are in my traveling coach with my valet. Never travel without the fellow; quite indispensable, you know."

"Of course," the viscount said smoothly. "If your groom will be so good as to take charge of my horse and take it round back with him, I shall show you inside and direct Thompson to escort you to a guest room."

"Well, well, that is kind of you," Holwell replied with genuine gratification. "I begin to believe my fears ungrounded, after all."

With exquisite restraint, Stanwood refrained from asking just what those fears might have been. Instead he bowed to Holwell and led the way inside, where he gave the necessary orders. Then, turning to Holwell, he said, "You will, I know, excuse me. I, too, have a distaste of greeting visitors in my riding dirt."

Stanwood then grimly retreated to his own suite of rooms.

Theodosia, never one to run from unpleasant situations, reached the drawing room well before either the viscount, or Helena, or Holwell. Alone there, she looked about the fashionable room and tried to picture the woman who had furnished it. A bit flighty, no doubt, for everything had been purchased with an eye to appearance and none to practicality. A woman who cared more for appearance than substance. Well, that was how Bartram had described his mother. Bartram! Theodosia caught herself abruptly. He was, he must be, to her, Lord Stanwood or at the very least Stanwood. Nothing had given her, nothing would give her, the right to call him Bartram.

And yet, she acknowledged silently, he had somehow become Bartram to her. Something about the man made her want to smooth away his cares and yet at the same time let him smooth away hers. Quite an impertinence, she thought, given that he sees me as no more than a flighty chit like his sister. Or if not quite that, certainly there is not the least trace of warmth in his manner toward me. And that was, she realized, the most lowering reflection of all.

It did not occur to her that a fine sense of propriety would have kept the viscount from revealing his feelings, no matter what they might be, to a young guest in Theodosia's position.

Holwell found her there in the drawing room looking out the window at the long expanse of green lawn that stretched down from the front of the house. "Lady Theodosia," he said with exquisite politeness, "how delightful it is to see you again. The country air has wrought a change that I had not thought possible."

Quickly Theodosia turned. Advancing with a hand held out to greet Holwell, she rallied him, "What? Such an antidote I must have been, then."

"Never!" he retorted fervently as he took her hand and held it for just the prescribed moment. Then, relaxing, he wagged a finger at her. "Now, now, you are roasting me. *Such* a sense of levity makes you all the more delightful, Lady Theodosia."

"Why, thank you, Sir Thomas. Tell me, why have you come to Stanwood Oaks? Business affairs with the viscount, perhaps?" she parried.

He raised his eyebrows a moment, then replied,

"You might say so, although to be frank, the matter concerns you."

"Me?" Theodosia laughed uneasily. "Whatever can you mean?"

Holwell placed his hands on the back of a chair. leaned forward, and said very deliberately, "I mean, Lady Theodosia, that when I learned from your grandmother that you were here with the viscount, lacking any proper chaperon, I was shocked. My concern led me, in fact, to come and assure myself that you were quite all right."

Her cheeks flushed, Theodosia retorted hotly, "To assure yourself that I had not embroiled myself in some sort of scandal, you mean?"

"No, no, of course not!" Holwell replied, shocked. "Only that matters appeared so irregular, and you are, after all, so young and inexperienced."

"I see. Well, you were much mistaken, Sir Thomas. There is nothing irregular here, after all," Theodosia told him bluntly. "I am well chaperoned, for my friend Helena's cousin Roberta looks after us quite well."

"Does she?" Holwell asked politely. "Then where is she now? It is most irregular for you to receive me alone, and a proper chaperon would not have allowed it."

At that precise moment a high querulous voice could be heard saying, "Alone? Improper. Most improper. I shall go in there at once."

Hastily Theodosia told Holwell, "You see? You were mistaken. And in any event, I am not receiving a morning call from you, for I understand we are now both houseguests here. Surely that alters matters somewhat?"

Holwell contented himself with giving Theodosia a speaking glance before turning to greet Miss Roberta Stanwood. He did so with his usual grace, and before long she had changed her expression from one of suspicious disapproval to one of hesitant acceptance. A trifle breathlessly she said, "You have come all the way from Bath to pay us a visit? Or rather Lady Theodosia? How romantic!" With a slight giggle she added, "Ah, but I shouldn't say that. I am putting you to the blush, sir."

At the sight of Holwell's affronted expression, Theodosia was hard put to bite back her laughter. With commendable self-control, however, she was able to say with only the slightest quaver to her voice, "Indeed, you must not say so, Miss Stanwood! You might very well be mistaken in the matter."

"What matter?" Helena demanded abruptly as she entered the drawing room without ceremony.

With no little asperity in his voice, Holwell replied, "I should be grateful if everyone would stop contemplating aloud what is none of their affair! My reasons for coming to the Oaks are *not* to be bandied about."

"Oh, dear, dear," Roberta stammered timidly, "we had no notion to offend you. Oh, dear, no, that would never do."

At the sight of the elderly Miss Stanwood's confusion, Holwell relented somewhat and said more mildly, "Forgive me, Miss Stanwood, I have had a long and tiring journey. I assure you I am not offended. I would, however, prefer to change the subject and talk of something else. Lady Theodosia, how have you kept yourself busy here? It must be a quiet change from Bath."

"Indeed, such a gay round of dissipation *that* was," Helena observed.

Theodosia shot her friend a warning look, but before she could speak, Roberta was earnestly answering Holwell, "You must not think us entirely isolated from society, here, Sir Thomas! Why, only tomorrow we are invited to dine with a very distinguished country family. Perhaps you have heard of them: the Cranleys?"

Holwell considered the matter before replying, "Why, yes, I believe their pedigree is a respectable one, though not outstanding, mind you. Still, one does not see them in London."

"That is because they are a most respectable family," Helena explained with a serious expression, "and would never put pleasure before duty. They do have rather extensive property to manage, you know." Holwell looked at her sharply, but Helena was the picture of innocence as she added, "You know, I've just had a notion! I shall send round a note to Clarissa asking if we may bring along Sir Thomas tomorrow night. I don't doubt she would be delighted."

Before Holwell could object, Helena was gone from the room and was left to express his misgivings to Theodosia, who was inclined to agree with him. That came from a lack of knowledge of Miss Clarissa Cranley, for her positive response

was to come in that same day. At the moment,
however, Helena's notion merely seemed a hare-
brained scheme. Only Roberta sounded a sensible
note as she said, "My mama was used to say that
an extra gentleman could never be other than a
welcome sight. Particularly a well-mannered and
eligible extra gentleman."

The simultaneous appearance of Stanwood, the
tea tray, and Helena made a change of conversation imperative. Bartram was at his best, talking
of all the things gentlemen find vastly entertain-
ing, and yet not excluding the ladies. To Helena
and Theodosia, who could not keep their minds
off the journal, it was an intolerable half-hour.
Even Cousin Roberta seemed a trifle restless, and
all three seemed to greet with relief Stanwood's
signal that teatime was over.

10

Setting down his teacup and rising to his feet, Stanwood said, "You will excuse me, I know—I have business to attend to."

"Wait!" Helena said, rising to *her* feet. "I thought you wanted to see the journal."

Stanwood regarded his sister grimly and then shrugged. "Very well. My affairs can wait a few minutes. Where is this journal?"

Helena and Theodosia exchanged speaking glances; then Helena said, "I shall go get it."

Silently Stanwood watched her go. "Journal?" Holwell asked. "A family matter, perhaps? Ought Lady Theodosia and I to excuse ourselves?"

The corner of Stanwood's mouth twitched, though whether from amusement or annoyance, Theodosia could not have said. "There is no need," he told Holwell curtly. "This is all nonsense, I don't doubt. My sister believes she has found a secret journal of my Grandfather's, that is all."

"All?" Theodosia demanded indignantly.

"Nonsense?" Cousin Roberta demanded equally indignantly. "There is no nonsense about it at all. Your grandfather was a great one for writing journals, or so he told me. And if it is about his China journey, you ought to be very interested. I am sure you will find it most enlightening and educational."

"*If* my grandfather ever went to China," Stanwood replied.

Surprisingly, it was Holwell who said, "He did." Three astonished pairs of eyes turned to Sir Thomas, who added, "My father said that he recalled your grandfather boasting at his clubs that he had a surprise in store for everyone and that in China, at least, his talents had been appreciated."

Frowning, Stanwood said, "Why, then, have I never heard the story? And why did my parents not know of it?"

Holwell waved a hand carelessly. "Oh, well, everyone thought your grandfather a mere braggart, and after a few months he ceased to speak of it. No one wished to hurt the family by passing on tales that must only have made him look absurd or worse. Besides, none of your grandfather's friends were ever on such terms with your father as would allow them to speak of it."

"I see," Stanwood said grimly. "Then why do you speak of it now?"

Again Holwell waved his hand. "Oh, well, if your sister has indeed found a journal that details his trip to China, then that changes everything.

He was not merely hiding out on the Continent and then telling tales to cover his disgrace. I should be very interested to hear what the journal says myself."

Just at that moment Helena returned and handed her brother a large bound volume.

"Is this it?" he asked curtly.

"Yes, Grandfather's journal!" she said a trifle breathlessly. "At least, the first one I could find. There are others, but I have not yet had the chance to look for them. This is the one that he wrote when he was sent out in exile."

"I see." His tone was not inviting. "And this describes what?"

"It starts with a brief explanation of how he got involved with the Jacobins and the Pretender and how he was put under interdict and was shipped out of the country. With the smugglers who operated right off the coast here," Helena explained excitedly. Almost as an afterthought she added, "And how he planned to be a pirate."

"Pirate?" Holwell exclaimed in astonishment.

Cousin Roberta tittered. "A pirate! How absurd. No, your grandfather was never a pirate, my dear. Whatever else he may have done, he was not that foolish. But the Pretender, you say? Yes, he did tell me he had had a difficult time as a youth, that he backed the wrong man. Such a romantic!" she concluded with a sigh. "A most unusual man."

"So it would seem," Holwell agreed dryly, "though a surprisingly foolish one."

"Foolish one?" Cousin Roberta was indignant.

"Not a bit of it! You forget he came back with a fortune from China."

"A fortune?" Holwell's eyebrows rose in astonishment.

"Some money, certainly," Bartram interjected sensibly, "for he made a number of changes, including the gardens designed by Repton. And he must have found the money on his own for my great-grandfather lost most of the family's funds prior to that, during the South Sea Bubble. That was, however, the extent of the fortune."

Cousin Roberta sniffed. "Believe whatever you like. *I* know what *he* told me."

Soothingly Stanwood replied, "Yes, yes, well I shall know better after I have read the journals. All of them. Nella, please go and bring the rest."

"But I don't know where they are," Helena replied with surprise. "I thought you understood. This is the only one we have found. In the beginning of this one, however, Grandfather states that he left an earlier journal in the library."

"Then let us repair there at once," Bartram said with a slight frown.

As one, the three ladies and two gentlemen left the drawing room and trooped down the hall to the library. Once there, Bartram reached for the volume his sister held in her hand. She opened it for him to the relevant page. " 'Fifth bookcase from the glass doors, top row, third volume from the end, amidst the Greeks,' " he read aloud.

Immediately Theodosia was on her way to the proper bookcase, reaching along the proper shelf looking for the book. After a few moments her fingers found it, noting by the feel of the binding how it differed from the others beside it. At once Helena gave a crow of triumph and reached for it. Bartram's fingers were the quicker.

"I'm sorry," he said with a smile that was oddly endearing as he took the volume away from Theodosia. "By rights, the two of you ought to get to see it first, but I do wish to get to the bottom of this myself."

In spite of herself, Theodosia returned the smile. "So I should hope. But I warn you, we shan't give you long with the things before we demand our turn at searching the journals for clues!"

Rising to her feet, Cousin Roberta said with a distinct sniff, "Searching the journals for clues indeed! As though my uncle would have been so careless as to leave the information so easy to find. Play at the game if you will, but excuse me from joining you. *I* have things to do."

In spite of her words, Cousin Roberta seemed in no real haste to leave, and indeed she brushed quite close to them all as she made her way out of the room.

The others stared after her and then Stanwood turned his pointed attention on Holwell, who hastily stammered, "Yes, well, I shall excuse myself as well. Are you coming, Lady Theodosia?"

"Soon," she replied, scarcely able to conceal her impatience.

Displeased, he nevertheless went.

When he was gone, Helena told her brother

warningly, "You shan't have that journal for long, Bartram. And if I did not have to go to the stables straightaway, I should dispute you for it now. One of the mares is about to drop a colt, however, and I am needed. No, stay, Dosie, there is no need for you to accompany me."

Left alone with the viscount, Theodosia found herself unaccountably restless. She also rose, intending to leave, but Stanwood echoed his sister's words. "No, stay a moment. There is something I wanted to speak to you about. I understand you have been in the kitchens talking with Cook, and in the stillroom. May I ask why?"

Theodosia colored but met his eyes squarely. "Nella showed me about everywhere, including the kitchens. It occurred to me that though your parents spent a great deal sprucing up the rest of the house, including this room, there was little done in the kitchens. Surely you have noticed that the meats are not always browned as they ought to be or the sauces quite smooth or the bread as high as one could wish. Well, I spoke with your cook to discover her opinion of the problem."

"And?" Stanwood asked grimly.

Theodosia weighed her words carefully. "And I think you would find your comfort greatly enhanced were you to install a Rumford stove. A really modern one, I mean."

"And where am I to find the money for that?" he asked sarcastically. "You must know the state we are in. I don't even know where I shall find the funds for Nella's dowry."

Carefully placing her fingertips together, Theodosia answered, "Over a year's time you will discover that the savings in food not burned or otherwise miscooked to go a long way toward paying the cost of the stove. You need not spend a fortune on one and you will find that suitors who are well fed will be far more likely to overlook Nella's lack of portion than those who are illtempered from indigestion."

For a moment matters hung in the balance, and then the viscount laughed. After several moments he wiped his eyes and looked at Theodosia, who regarded him with perfect equanimity. "And the stillroom? I suppose you have advice there, as well?"

"Not advice," she countered, "merely a request. You are sadly lacking in a number of things that are handy to have about the house. I wondered if you would mind if I used the stillroom. There are various tonics and restoratives and such that I should like to prepare." He looked at her astounded, and Theodosia added a trifle anxiously, "I like to work in the stillroom, you see. For me it is a . . . a soothing occupation."

Stanwood did not at once reply. Instead he regarded her steadily for several moments, his expression grave. At last he said, "You are . . . what, a year older than my sister?" She nodded and he went on, "Yet you speak as someone who has long run a large household. How is this?"

Theodosia found it surprisingly difficult to answer him. She looked down at her hands as she said, "You have said that you know something of the Elston reputation. Well, it is true, much of it. My mother and father were not ones to bury themselves in the country. Someone had to take a hand in running the estate. From an early age, of course, I was at school in Bath most of the year. But on holidays and such I tried to put aright what neglect had disarranged. Particularly after my mother left for the Americas. My father, you see, liked his comfort, and we were all happier if he was." With a slight smile she said, "The stove made the greatest difference, I think. But now my brother is installed there with his wife, and my talents are not needed. And yet, it is foolish of me, I know, but I miss the stillroom the most. My grandmother in Bath has neither the patience nor the room for one in her establishment."

With a lightness he did not feel, the viscount replied, "Well, Lady Theodosia, you are quite welcome to use mine as much as you like. And perhaps I shall purchase that stove."

The pallor had left Theodosia's face and her eyes twinkled as she replied, "One's stomach always wins out."

"Do you know," the viscount told her disconcertingly, "I am beginning to be very grateful I brought you along to be with Nella, even if you are something of a mystery to me." Then abruptly he turned serious. "Lady Theodosia, is there anything to what Miss Cranley said? That Nella has been riding out alone? Perhaps to . . . to meet with someone? I am sure you will not be surprised to hear that she was meeting someone clandestinely in Bath. Someone who even posed as me."

Theodosia colored. "I . . . I did hear of the incident in Bath," she said faintly. "But I assure you Nella is riding out to meet no one here. If she is indiscreet, it is only in the wildness of the gallops she takes, and I cannot but think that a relatively harmless way for her to work off her energy. That and her search for this 'treasure.' "

"And Devere?" Stanwood persisted. "You see, I already know his name. Can you tell me for certain that he has not followed my sister here?"

Theodosia swallowed hard as she replied. "I . . . I have not seen him here. Indeed, I myself have some acquaintance of him and can assure you that when I last spoke with him . . . in Bath . . . he had no intention of following Nella here."

At Theodosia's words the viscount frowned. "You know Devere as well? I am surprised. There was no one in Bath who could tell me who he was." A sudden thought occurred to him, and Stanwood said severely, "He is of the *ton*, is he not? Or has my sister taken up with tradesmen or dancing masters or such?"

Coloring, Theodosia hastily turned away. "Oh, certainly Devere is of the *ton*. Your sister has too much pride for it to be otherwise."

"But insufficient pride," Stanwood countered grimly, "to refuse a clandestine affair with a man odious enough to pose as another to gain her chaperon's confidence." Theodosia did not answer, and he went on, "You are silent. Did you also have a fondness for this Devere? Is he, perhaps, the reason your grandmother consented to have you accompany my sister to the country? Is that the reason Holwell must charge to your defense? Because he is aware you have a weakness for such men and thought I might be one as well?"

With a sigh Theodosia turned and faced the viscount once more. Meeting his eyes squarely, she said, "I have no interest in Devere. Nor, I think, does Nella any longer. Indeed, it was never more than a lark for her to see him at all. The rest of your accusations are too odious to answer. I will only repeat that I see no harm in Nella's behavior here. Wild gallops and a search for the treasure are her current passion."

"Do you truly think the treasure exists?" Stanwood asked curiously.

"I think it does not matter, but certainly to discover a treasure would help your financial position. Even if you do not, however, it is one way of diverting Nella from other, perhaps less innocuous notions."

The viscount looked at her steadily. "I think, perhaps, I was right after all. You are a good influence on Nella, and I am most pleased that I brought you here," he said. And then, before Theodosia could decide what to say, he added, "Now I am sure you will be good as to leave me alone. I wish to read these journals."

With what little composure Theodosia could muster, she nodded and gratefully fled the room.

11

The household at the Oaks kept country hours, and it was shortly past eight when Theodosia entered the breakfast room the next morning. The curtains had been drawn back and sunlight flooded the room. Strangers stared at Theodosia from every angle, from framed portraits on the walls to the Romans on the painted ceiling. With the equanimity born of having eaten in such rooms most of her life, she ignored them. Viscount Stanwood and Sir Thomas were already present and she greeted them with a nod before filling her plate at the sideboard.

"You have an excellent appetite, I see," Stanwood said dryly.

With perfect composure Theodosia seated herself, smoothing the sprigged-muslin fabric of her dress as she did so. "I do not hold that one should starve oneself when one has a full day of activities planned," she replied calmly.

"Sensible," Holwell said a trifle pompously.

Ignoring his other guest, Stanwood asked
Theodosia, "And just what *do* you have planned
for today?"

Theodosia was about to answer when Helena
entered the room. Words spilled out of her in a
rush. "Where are the journals, Bartram?" she
demanded. "You must have known we would
want to see them again!"

Calmly Stanwood finished drinking from his
teacup before he replied maddeningly, "That
dress no longer becomes you, Nella. We really
must see about refurbishing your wardrobe—if
the estate can stand the expense."

At any other time such a pronouncement would
have garnered Helena's full attention and
brought forth from her both indignation and
delight. At the moment, however, she was not to
be diverted. "I asked you about the journals,"
she repeated, tapping her foot.

Bartram frowned. "So you did. And I don't
know what the devil you are talking about.
Grandfather's journals should be right where I
left them—on my desk in the library."

"Well, they are not," Helena retorted impatiently.

"*What?*" the viscount thundered. "Impossible!
I left them both together there. If you are
roasting us, Nella, I take leave to tell you that I
find it a very poor jest."

"Roasting you?" Nella gasped with
indignation. "How dare you think such a thing?"

"How dare you accuse me of such perfidy as
hiding the journals?" her brother countered.

Knowing very well her friend's fiery temper, Theodosia judged it time to intervene. "I suggest that directly after we have eaten we repair to the library and look for the journals," she said calmly.

"*After* we have eaten?" Helena protested.

Theodosia met her friend's eyes with a smile. "Why not? Do you expect something else to occur while we eat? Perhaps they will reappear. In any event, I, for one, do not intend to starve."

"Nor do I," Stanwood added promptly.

"You are both of you entirely unfeeling," Helena charged indignantly.

"But eminently sensible," Holwell pointed out.

Helena sniffed but nevertheless proceeded to fill her plate. As she sat down, she asked with a frown, "Where is Cousin Roberta? In Bath she was always a stickler for early rising."

"She still is," Bartram confirmed with a smile. "She was already finishing her breakfast when I came down for mine. Said she intended to go for an invigorating walk and then take charge of the gardener, who she says has been making a shocking muddle of some of the shrubberies."

"*Poor* Humphrey," Helena said with feeling.

Stanwood laughed. "Scarcely, my dear Nella! I have no doubt that Humphrey will give as good as he gets. All he needs tell her is that he is honoring the memory of my dear mother and continuing to fulfill her wishes, and what can Cousin Roberta answer to that?"

"She'll think of something," Helena said with a delicate shudder.

"Meanwhile," Theodosia pointed out calmly, "we don't have her in our hair while we try to sort out this mess about the journals. She is a dear lady but rather muddleheaded at times, I'm afraid."

With an attempt to humor, Holwell said, "Perhaps you will think me a nuisance as well, Lady Theodosia. For I intend to join you in unraveling this mystery, you see. But at least I may pride myself that you would not call *me* muddleheaded."

Helena started to speak but hastily fell silent at the minatory look Bartram directed at her, so no one contradicted Sir Thomas.

Directly after breakfast, the four repaired to the library. The journals were precisely where Stanwood had left them. Leveling a compelling stare upon his sister, he said, "I told you I thought it a poor jest."

"But I wasn't jesting," Helena protested helplessly. "They *were* gone when I looked half an hour ago."

"Perhaps one of the maids moved them when she dusted," Theodosia suggested sensibly. "In any case, I cannot see that it matters now that we have found them again. How far did you get in reading them, Stanwood?"

"Far enough," he replied grimly. "My grandfather was quite a fellow, and I do *not* think his journal appropriate reading for young ladies. He was indeed involved in the Jacobin rebellion, and much more. Even before his hasty escape from

England, he seems to have had a penchant for secrecy. He hid his first journal here in the library, and in it he mentions another favorite hiding place."

"Where?" Helena pounced breathlessly.

The viscount smiled wryly. "In the ruins, though the thought of him climbing about out there is difficult to credit."

"The ruins?" Helena asked. "Do you mean where . . . where Jeremy died?"

Puzzled, Stanwood nodded. "Yes, but what is that to the point?"

"Don't you see?" Nella asked breathlessly. "Perhaps he was searching for the treasure also!"

"It scarcely seems likely," Stanwood said witheringly. "Why would he not have told us what he was about? And how would he have known to look for a treasure at all?"

"What if he had found the journal, quite by accident, and tried to look for the secret spot Grandfather wrote about? You weren't here for him to tell, and he never confided in me anyway," Helena persisted. "And perhaps when he was searching the ruins, he slipped and fell."

"Most unlikely," the viscount replied, "and in any event, we shall never know, so I find it useless to speculate upon the matter."

Unable to suppress a shudder, Theodosia said suspiciously, "I suppose you mean to go there and search all by yourself?"

"I had thought of doing so," Stanwood admitted meekly, "but recognized that it was an act you two would scarcely approve. Therefore, if you can be ready in half an hour, you may come along with me."

Grimly Theodosia said, "We shall meet you at the stables, and in less than half an hour, I assure you!" Then, before he could retract his offer, the two girls fled to their chambers. With a sigh of resignation Stanwood went up to his.

The viscount reached the stables no more than twenty-five minutes later, but his sister, Lady Theodosia, and Holwell had all preceded him. The ladies had already mounted and Sir Thomas was preparing to do so. As Stanwood watched, Holwell easily swung into his saddle and Helena said teasingly, "What? Taken so long, Bartram? We were about to leave without you."

"Ah, but you forget you need me," he retorted, mounting onto the horse his groom held ready. "Or rather my knowledge."

Nella tossed her head. "Oh, pooh! I daresay we would have found the spot without you."

"Well, then, when we reach the ruins," Stanwood retorted, "you may spend as much time looking as you please before I tell you the secret."

In her quietly amused voice Theodosia broke in to say, "Peace, Nella! I for one do not plan to spend the entire day looking for what your brother may discover in a few moments."

"Thank you," he said, turning on his guest a smile.

It was a smile, Theodosia thought, in sharp contrast to the worry about his eyes, a worry she found herself wanting to smooth away. And that, she told herself sharply as she bent her head to pat her horse's neck, is quite enough nonsense out of you, my girl!

It was Holwell who spoke aloud and said, "Do we mean to sit here all day or shall we be on our way?"

"By all means let us go," the viscount retorted curtly, and turning his horse, added, "This way, toward the coast."

Holwell somehow found the opportunity to edge his horse next to Theodosia's. "I confess I cannot quite believe in this mysterious treasure," he told her with a kindly smile, "but no more can I bring myself to spoil the sense of adventure your friend undoubtedly feels."

Theodosia smiled, finding herself in charity with Sir Thomas. "I agree," she said confidingly. "It has been hard for Nella, this past year, with the loss of her parents and the time spent in mourning and now buried away here in the countryside. If this nonsensical hunt gives her a change from all that, then so much the better."

"You are a kind friend," Holwell observed. As she colored, he continued, "It is one of the things I quite like about you, Lady Theodosia. You are kindhearted, never above your company, and inevitably a charming companion. These are qualities I find difficult to resist, my dear."

It was impossible to be offended or displeased by such kind words, and Theodosia was not. Indeed, she found herself feeling far more in charity with him than she ever had in Bath. Perhaps that was why she found it so easy to laugh at the *on-dit* he shared with her, drawing the viscount and Nella's speculative eyes to the pair.

In what seemed no time to Theodosia and Holwell, and forever to Stanwood, the three reached the ruins. Stanwood tethered their horses and the four made their way on foot.

"Why here?" Theodosia asked as they walked toward the ruins. "It seems such an inconvenient place."

"Perhaps that's why," Bartram retorted. "Persons from the house would never see what Grandfather was about. Nor think to search here themselves."

With a mischievous grin Helena added, "If they did see Grandfather here, they might have mistaken him for a ghost haunting the ruins."

"That or a free trader looking for a place to store his goods, perhaps," Theodosia suggested.

Stanwood shook his head. "No. It's well known around here that the free traders use certain caves and one or two barns, as well as a church some miles away. They've no need for a place as unsheltered as these ruins. But someone appears to have taken an interest now," he said grimly as he suddenly spied a flash of black cloth ahead of them.

Ignoring the others, he strode ahead, reaching out for the cloth, when suddenly he halted in astonishment. *"Cousin Roberta?"* he said.

Theodosia and Helena were not far behind Stanwood and they too regarded Miss Stanwood with astonishment. She returned their stare a trifle nearsightedly as she stammered, "Wh-why, Lord Stanwood! Whatever are you doing here?

And where am I? I meant to go looking for that nice berry patch on your land, but all I found were a few poor specimens. And then I saw this place. I do recall there were some ruins on your grandfather's land, but I thought they were in quite the opposite direction."

Helena directed a speaking look at Theodosia and her brother, hard pressed to conceal her amusement. Stanwood's voice was merely kind, however, as he replied, "You *have* got turned around, cousin. Why not give it up until tomorrow, for the patch you mean is a good mile or more away."

"Well, I ought not to, but I shall," Cousin Roberta replied, her voice quavering slightly. "I *still* must speak to your gardener about his work, you know. And my feet *are* tired."

"Why don't you sit down over here and rest?" Theodosia suggested, pointing to some stones that formed a natural bench.

Roberta did so, ignoring the angry look Helena directed at Theodosia. Indeed, apparently oblivious of all of them, Cousin Roberta closed her eyes. Helena looked helplessly at her brother, who merely shrugged.

"Well, shall we get on with it?" Holwell asked impatiently.

The earlier Stanwood must have given very precise directions in his journal for locating the hiding place, for it took Bartram no more than ten minutes to find the right stone and remove it. Inside was a strongbox, now rusted with age. Carefully Bartram drew it out and set it down on a nearby rock. "We shall have to pry it open," he said after examining it carefully.

Suddenly a voice behind the three startled them. "Rubbish? Rubbish in the ruins? Whatever would Uncle Henry have said?"

Stanwood turned to face his cousin and replied politely, "That is why we shall take it away from here. As you say, Grandfather would have been most distressed to have seen this lying about."

"I should think so!" Roberta sniffed. Then, a trifle suspiciously, "What's in the box?"

"I don't know," Stanwood told her. "I shall know better when I have taken it home and opened it. We haven't got the key, you see."

Helena, who had been fiddling with the box, suddenly announced, "We don't need the key! I've got it open."

"*What?*" three voices exclaimed simultaneously.

"I don't know how, but I've got it open," she repeated.

"My dear Nella, I do believe I've underrated you," Theodosia said, half to herself.

"Most irregular," Holwell said disapprovingly.

"Nonsense! Utter rubbish!" Roberta said as she, too, leaned closer.

Stanwood merely reached for the box and pried it the rest of the way. Inside were several sheets of paper with faded writing on them, a set of keys, and a number of small trinkets made of porcelain and some of carved jade.

"So he really did go to China," Holwell said with little surprise.

"That's what I told you," Roberta sniffed offendedly.

"So you did," Stanwood replied soothingly.

"Now what do we do?" Theodosia asked quietly.

"Go back to the house and look all of this over," he replied at once.

"Sensible, sensible," Holwell observed judiciously.

With an air of injured dignity, Cousin Roberta backed away and said with a sniff, "You may choose to spend your time on such nonsense if you wish. *I* have better things to do."

Astonished, Helena said, "But you are the one who insisted Grandfather hid a treasure somewhere on the estate!"

Roberta sniffed again. "So he did say. And if you choose to believe in such nonsense, that is your affair."

And with that she started to walk away. Behind her the others looked at one another in disbelief. Theodosia was the first to recover. "Wait!" she called out. "Don't you want to ride one of the horses back to the house?"

Cousin Roberta shook her head. "Can't abide the creatures; never could." She sighed, then added, "It was the one thing that displeased my uncle. But I could not and would not change, and I am not about to begin now." And with that pronouncement she once more began to pick her way homeward.

Helena shrugged. "Let her go, Dosie. If she wants to walk, let her."

Troubled, Theodosia nevertheless had no choice but to agree. And with the others she remounted her horse and they returned to the stables and then to the main house at Stanwood Oaks.

12

At the house the group was greeted with the information that there was a major crisis in the kitchen, that the upstairs maid was upset over several torn sheets just discovered, and that the viscount's new bailiff was waiting in the library. A look of intense weariness crossed Stanwood's face, and Theodosia found herself saying, "Nella and I will speak to Cook immediately, *and* the maid. I've no doubt there is some silly misunderstanding and we shall be able to set everything right in a trice."

Nella started to protest, but one look at her friend's face silenced her. Stanwood hesitated, then smiled at Theodosia. "Thank you," he said warmly. "I doubt the bailiff has good news, but I find him easier to deal with than Cook when she is in one of her tempers."

Theodosia waved a hand. "Never mind. We shall deal with her."

Stanwood excused himself and headed for the

library, strongbox still clamped securely under
one arm. Theodosia watched him go, then turned
to Holwell. "You will excuse us, I know," she said
with a smile.

He looked at her, troubled, and said after a
moment, "Lady Theodosia, may I speak with you
alone?"

"Without a chaperon?" she teased him kindly.

Holwell continued to look troubled, however,
and Helena said hastily, "Of course you may, Sir
Thomas. Dosie, I shall be in the kitchen with
Cook."

Theodosia nodded, and they watched Helena
leave. Then Holwell said, "Lady Theodosia, I
don't mean to criticize, and I know you have a
kind heart. And yet . . . well, do you think it wise
to be so involved in the day-to-day affairs of Lord
Stanwood's estate?"

"What . . . what do you mean?" Theodosia
asked, genuinely puzzled.

Holwell hesitated. "It must look . . . it *does* look
very particular that you are managing
Stanwood's domestic affairs for him."

It was Theodosia's turn to be troubled. "But
that is not the case at all. Indeed, in other circumstances one might say so, but surely not
here? Helena is my dearest friend and this is her
home as well as Lord Stanwood's. And, in
general, the housekeeper manages everything
perfectly well."

"But not today," Holwell persisted gently.
"My dear Theodosia, I only fear that you are
being too much imposed upon."

For a long moment Theodosia stared at the floor before she finally said, "I cannot answer you, Sir Thomas, save to say that I will not abandon my friends when there is difficulty, whether the problem is domestic or otherwise. I would not be myself if I did. And now you must excuse me. There is a cook who needs to be soothed. Mrs. Thompson must have gone out to market." Holwell bowed and let her pass. As she did, Theodosia paused to add with a mischievous smile, "You ought to be glad I cannot keep from interfering. Otherwise your stay would be marked by burned meals and damp sheets, and I cannot help but feel that you would find that a most unpleasant experience."

In the kitchen Theodosia found Helena trying to soothe the tempers of both the cook and the upstairs maid. Neither was in a mood to be pleased.

"I'm sure I don't know how I am to prepare decent meals when—"

"The sheets, ma'am, they've got such tears, and I swear they weren't there a week ago—"

"Mrs. Thompson is forever telling us—"

"And I did tell her that we would need—"

"It's always like this," Helena whispered to her friend, "when Mrs. Thompson is gone for the day."

It was some time before Theodosia escaped, having calmed down both the cook and the maid and promised to help with the mending herself. Helena had long since disappeared and Theodosia found she wanted nothing more than to go to her room and rest. In particular, she did not want to encounter Holwell!

Once in her room, Theodosia stood by the window, one finger idly tracing a pattern on the window ledge. She could not suppress the memory of a gallop on horseback outside of Bath. Not that there were no horses here! The viscount kept a fine stable, though much reduced since his parents died. Nor would anyone stop her if she chose to gallop. No, it was the memory of wearing men's riding breeches and the freedom one felt, dressed as a man, that Theodosia missed.

Not that she wished to be a man. She was not so foolish as to think that being a man made everything right. No, she only wished that women were not so hemmed about with rules and restrictions. It would be such a relief to stride freely about and do as she wished, as men did, for however short a time! But that was impossible here at Stanwood Oaks.

I am fortunate, Theodosia told herself dryly, that I did not bring those clothes from Bath, for otherwise I fear I should make a scandal of myself straightaway! Holwell, who is forever speaking of propriety and such, makes me feel so trapped that I find myself caring nothing for my name. Which is a most foolish position, I know, she acknowledged silently. But when will he leave?

If he leaves, Theodosia amended. She knew very well that he had come to Stanwood Oaks to be with her, and she could not help wondering if he were already making plans as to where he and she might go, whom they might see, after they were wed. It was the sort of thing one might expect of him, for he would be unable to conceive that she might spurn him.

At that moment there was a knock at Theodosia's door and she started. Hastily she crossed the room and opened her door. There stood Helena, who said impatiently, "Let's go find my brother and see what was in the box!"

Without hesitation Theodosia agreed, and a few moments later they were headed for the library with scarcely suppressed excitement. Once there, Helena knocked and walked in without waiting for a reply. To their astonishment, Theodosia and Helena found Stanwood and Holwell deep in conversation.

Staunchly Helena marched forward. "Where is Grandfather's box?" she demanded.

"Did you read the papers? What do they say?" Theodosia added a trifle more calmly than her friend.

"Was there a secret compartment?" Helena demanded.

"In a strongbox?" Stanwood asked his sister witheringly. "No, you saw what was there. And, yes, I did take time to look quickly over the papers inside the box."

"But where is the box?" Helena repeated.

"In my room, in a safe place," Bartram told her austerely. "I thought it best not to drag it about with me."

"I want to see it," Helena replied stubbornly.

"And so you shall," he agreed. "Tomorrow."

"Tomorrow?" Helena protested. "Why not today? Right now?"

"I said tomorrow," Bartram repeated. "Now, do you want to know what was in the papers?"

"Yes!" Theodosia said before Helena could protest further.

Stanwood paused, then said with a flourish, "Directions to a secret room or rooms here at Stanwood Oaks."

"Preposterous," Holwell snorted.

"Where?" Helena demanded, ignoring Sir Thomas.

"That we shall find out tomorrow perhaps," he answered. "The directions are written in some sort of code, which must still be deciphered. And it's no use protesting, Nella, for we have a guest to entertain and a dinner party to prepare for."

Glowering, Helena stared from her brother to Holwell and back again. Suspiciously she asked, "What were you two talking about, then? Plans to search for the rooms without us?"

"Nella . . ." Stanwood began warningly.

"My dear Miss Stanwood," Holwell said stiffly, "I have no intention of becoming involved in your family affairs. If you so dislike my presence here, I shall refrain from even taking part in the search, which I am sure your brother will conduct in your presence. Though I must say—"

"What were you talking about, then?" Helena persisted.

Holwell colored, and had he not been the consummate gentleman, Theodosia had little doubt he would have given Helena a thorough dressing-down. Instead he left it to Stanwood to say, "Nella, it is a matter that does not concern you. Lady Theodosia perhaps, but not you, and we shall not discuss it with you! I suggest that you and Lady Theodosia go back upstairs and rest for this evening's dinner party."

"Rest!" Helena snorted.

"Don't you even want to know if your domestic problems were resolved?" Theodosia asked him provocatively.

For the first time since they had entered the room, Stanwood smiled. "With you to help, how can I doubt it?" he asked lightly.

Frowning, Helena said, "How do you know I did not resolve matters? You give me too little credit, you know."

"Do I?" he asked his sister dryly. "My apologies. When we set about finding a husband for you we shall have to be sure to list domestic skills as one of your excellent qualities."

"You are roasting me, and that is not kind of you," Helena retorted. "Come along, Dosie. Let us leave them to their nonsense."

Theodosia shrugged. "As you wish. I have a small tear in my dress to mend before this evening, in any event." At the door of the library she paused and looked back at the two gentlemen. "You said you would not tell Nella what you were both talking about. Does that apply to me as well?" The two men nodded, and she went on, "Very well, but you, Lord Stanwood, have already conceded it was of matters that perhaps concern me. I might have a few guesses then.

Just recollect that when you presume to dispose of my affairs that they *are* my affairs and no one may direct them but myself! Good day, gentlemen.''

13

Miss Clarissa Cranley awaited the arrival of her guests with no little trepidation. Her gown was a simple one of dark blue taffeta. She was *not* in mourning, though one might have been pardoned for thinking so, given her taste in clothing. No, it was simply that she considered pastel colors far too frivolous for someone possessed of such a mature turn of mind as her own. Nor was Clarissa's hair fashionably dressed. A simple knot at the top of her head sufficed, though the diamond drops at her ears and the slippers on her feet were of the finest quality.

Beside Miss Cranley stood her mother. Seeing the two together, no one could have doubted that Clarissa's firm determination forever outweighed Mrs. Cranley's timid nature. Indeed there were those who tended to forget that Mrs. Cranley existed, so visible was the daughter. Even now Mrs. Cranley nervously fingered the orange crepe of her gown with concern, wondering if Clarissa quite approved the color. But she had said it would be all right to replace the last one, now hopelessly worn, with something of the same sort.

Colonel Cranley meanwhile eyed his daughter with kindness but with a few misgivings of his own. This dinner party was none of his idea, but since Clarissa had chosen to give it, she might have chosen a more fashionable gown. Particularly as reports were that Stanwood's guest was a most attractive young lady. The colonel sighed but held his tongue. Experience had taught him that Clarissa listened to no counsel but her own. And in any event, he had already overheard his wife try to advise Clarissa on precisely the same matter, just that afternoon. Clarissa's reply had been typical of her: "He must take me as I am. If Stanwood is more attracted by a pretty dress than by a serious turn of mind, he is not the man I believe him to be."

The fourth occupant of the room, Peter Cranley, was less restrained. He could not resist roasting his sister constantly. "Did you give Cook *precise* instructions?" he asked with apparent seriousness. "One would not want her to take less offense than the last time you gave a dinner party. Are you quite certain we are fashionable enough for Stanwood and his guest? I understand him to be quite taken with her."

Through clenched teeth Clarissa replied, "This is a simple dinner party and they are not the only guests."

Peter waved a hand carelessly. "Yes, yes, I

know. The Wartons and Reverend Seeley and his wife are coming, but they scarcely count, and you know it."

"There is someone else as well!" she said defensively.

"Who?"

"Sir Thomas Holwell," Clarissa answered with an air of triumph.

Peter whistled. "Oh, ho! So that's the way it is, is it? A second swain in the wings in the event you've somehow whistled Stanwood down the wind? Or is Holwell to be a foil to try to arouse Stanwood's baser instincts—such as jealousy?"

Having had the tables turned so neatly on her, Clarissa answered angrily, "You have much mistaken the matter, Peter. Sir Thomas is also staying with Stanwood. Perhaps he is attached to Stanwood's sister."

Peter merely grinned. "A Holwell and a Stanwood? But we shall see," he said blandly, "we shall see."

There was no need to answer him, for at that moment the first of the guests was announced, the Reverend and Mrs. Seeley, followed immediately by the Wartons and the Stanwood party. Clarissa was all gracious courtesy as she welcomed them, standing with touching affection at her mother and father's side.

"Mrs. Seeley, how wonderful to have you here again," Clarissa said. "And you, as well, Reverend Seeley. Your sermon this past week was very inspiring."

"Actually Clarissa invited you to keep me

company," her father interjected heartily. "Knew I'd want to talk about this year's fishing and such. Plus a game of chess afterward."

"Papa!" Miss Cranley remonstrated.

Mrs. Seeley and Mrs. Cranley merely smiled warmly at one another, knowing that whatever else might occur, they, at least, would find the time to share the parish gossip together.

The reverend was not offended. He held up a hand and said amiably, "No, no, Miss Cranley, the only objection I have to your father's plan is that he never seems to show the proper respect for my calling when he proceeds to destroy me at chess!"

With a hearty chuckle the colonel waved Seeley on so that he could greet the Wartons. They were a young, rather unfashionable couple, but of impeccable breeding and friends from when they and Clarissa and Bartram had all been children. "Charles! Louise! How delightful to see you!" Clarissa said with genuine pleasure. "I am sure Stanwood will feel the same."

The couple looked at each other and smiled knowingly. "He *is* coming, then?" Louise asked delicately.

"Oh, yes, Stanwood and his sister and two houseguests," Clarissa replied airily.

"Devilishly fine-looking girl, I'm told," the colonel chimed in. "Don't know who the other guest is, though. Didn't know he had another houseguest."

"Sir Thomas Holwell," Clarissa replied tightly. Then, with an effort, she smiled again and added,

"You have been in London recently. I'm sure you must have seen him there."

"We have," Louise assured her friend. "He is one of London's more eligible gentlemen."

"Word had it he was casting his eyes in the direction of an Elston," Charles added helpfully.

"Indeed?" Clarissa brightened visibly at this information. "No doubt that is why both of them are Stanwood's houseguests just now."

Before the Wartons could reply, the Stanwood party was announced. With an effort Clarissa restrained herself from crossing the room. Instead she waited until the viscount and his party had crossed to her. She was most impressed with Sir Thomas Holwell and found herself wishing that there had been more people of stature in the area whom she could have invited to dinner. Stanwood introduced them and Clarissa said with a slight flutter, "Sir Thomas! You honor us by joining our little dinner party. I am sure you are accustomed to much more fashionable affairs."

With a natural grace Holwell bowed and then addressed, as was only proper, his hostess. "Mrs. Cranley, I must thank you for having been so kind as to allow me to join your party tonight. It cannot have been other than troublesome for you."

At this unexpected kindness, Mrs. Cranley colored and curtsied, saying with genuine warmth, "On the contrary, Sir Thomas, I cannot tell you how pleased we are to have you with us!"

Again Holwell bowed, and this time he

addressed Clarissa. "I assure you, Miss Cranley, that it is just such quiet little affairs that I prefer."

"Very neatly said." The colonel nodded approvingly.

As she watched, a thought occurred to Theodosia and she added helpfully, "Sir Thomas is being quite honest, Clarissa. His natural taste is such as to take offense at the overblown extravagances so popular in London these days. Indeed, I don't doubt you would find he far prefers your sobriety of dress to the frivolity of mine."

Had good manners not required that Holwell reassure Theodosia that he found her dress delightful, he would have been quite tempted to agree. She wore a confection of while silk and silver lace that was cut lower than he could think proper. She might at least have worn a shawl about her shoulders, he thought crossly. Ringlets of curls clustered about her face and emeralds dangled from her ears and about her throat. Even in London she might have been called slightly daring.

As it was, Holwell found himself exchanging a speaking look with this Miss Cranley, as Stanwood's sister said with an innocent air, "Yes, well, you have not had the time to outgrow such nonsense as Clarissa has."

At which point Stanwood conveniently espied the Wartons and the conversation became far more general. Nevertheless it could not be said that Holwell was entirely disappointed to find himself placed on Miss Cranley's right at the dinner table, from which vantage point he could watch Theodosia flirt outrageously with Charles Warton.

Nor could it be denied that Holwell was a trifle distracted by the sight of his hoped-to-be fiancée behave with such little reserve, and after two or three attempts at polite conversation Miss Cranley abandoned the attempt. Rather bluntly she said, "Is something the matter, Sir Thomas?"

Holwell smiled at Clarissa. She seemed a sensible young woman, and the one or two remarks he had heard had only confirmed this opinion. And so he somehow found himself confiding in her. Or rather, he began by confirming the shrewd guesses she made.

"Lady Theodosia seems a nice child," Clarissa said diffidently, "but in need of a strong guiding hand."

"She is, indeed," Holwell sighed, "though one cannot blame her, for her mother is never anywhere to be found, and I understand she has been much on her own these last few years."

"Such a pity," Clarissa said, "for I feel she has a good nature if she could only manage to rule her levity."

Again Holwell nodded. "But it is natural, I suppose, in one so young to see such a delight in all sorts of nonsensical things."

Clarissa sighed. "Alas, I have never understood that. Perhaps it is due to my own mother's careful upbringing, but I have always had far too many serious matters to concern myself with to care for endless parties and games and such."

"Indeed?" Holwell was all sympathetic interest.

Watching Miss Cranley and Holwell from the far corner of the table, Stanwood frowned. Whatever were Clarissa and Holwell finding to talk about so earnestly?

Eyeing the same pair, Theodosia and Helena exchanged mischievous smiles. Her grandmother would no doubt be angry if Holwell fixed his interest elsewhere, but it would serve her right for sending the fellow here, Theodosia thought crossly. She would not have been in the least disturbed had she known what they were talking about.

"I arrived," Holwell was saying, with a bluntness that would have astounded anyone who knew him, "expecting most naturally that Lady Theodosia would be pleased to see me, though not expecting her to forget herself so far as to show it. Instead I find her manners abrupt, her tongue far too ready to answer seriousness with levity, and something far too dashing in her attire."

"For that you must in part blame Miss Stanwood," Clarissa said. "I cannot help but think her influence on Lady Theodosia is not a good one. These things you say could describe Miss Stanwood in every way. What a pity you cannot take Lady Theodosia away from such an unfortunate influence."

"Well, I cannot," he replied shortly. "She has not yet given me the right to do so, nor has her family."

"But if you could, you would?" Clarissa asked, all but licking her lips.

"I would," he confirmed tightly.

"Then we must put our heads together and see what notions we can discover," she told him.

As though striking a bargain, the two nodded and turned back to the other guests. But Stanwood had long since ceased to watch them. His attention was drawn by the same sight that had captured Holwell's attention earlier: Theodosia flirting, but this time with Peter Cranley.

"I can scarcely credit you are Clarissa's brother," Theodosia said with a laugh. "You are so . . . so . . ."

"So frivolous? So mischievous?" Peter suggested helpfully. "You may be sure I hear that constantly. I am forever playing pranks, and when I do, it is not my father or even my mother, but rather Clarissa who lectures me about the matter! For example, if you were to agree to run off and elope with me tonight, it would be Clarissa, not my father, who would come after us."

Biting her lower lip, Theodosia looked about the table and then said, "I think there are others besides Clarissa who might come after us."

Following her gaze, Peter sobered slightly. "Ah, yes. Stanwood and your friend Holwell. They both look as though they should like to see me disappear."

With another laugh, Theodosia and Peter saluted one another with their glasses. After a moment Cranley said, a trifle seriously, "Tell me, do you know Holwell well?" Theodosia colored and Peter hastened to say, "Oh, I don't mean to distress you, it is just that I find it odd Holwell is Stanwood's guest. Odd, I mean, that he would come."

Theodosia bit her lower lip, wondering how frank she ought to be. At last she said with a laugh and a shrug of her shoulder, "As to that, I don't think my host invited him, I think he just came."

"How very odd," Peter repeated.

Her curiosity aroused, Theodosia said lightly, "Why? They are not, I think, close friends, but why should not one member of the *ton* visit another?"

"Sorry, I forgot you wouldn't know," Peter said sheepishly. "Stanwood's grandfather and Holwell's father got into quite a row years ago. Holwell's father thought the old viscount had cheated him somehow, I understand."

"But surely Stanwood's grandfather would have been far older than Holwell's father," Theodosia protested. "They could not have moved in the same circles."

Cranley shrugged. "They did not. It was a business matter, originally negotiated by Holwell's grandfather, but when he died Holwell's father took over. That's why I find it odd to see Holwell here and on such apparent good terms with Stanwood. Not that Bartram ain't a likable guy."

He grinned, and Theodosia returned it, then

turned the talk to lighter matters. Soon they were both laughing again. Almost at once Clarissa rose, suggesting that the ladies retire from the table and leave the gentlemen to their brandy.

Once in the drawing room, Clarissa turned to Theodosia and said, "I know you won't take it amiss, Lady Theodosia, if I warn you that my brother is a flighty fellow and you ought not to attend to what he says. Even when he has been *most* particular in his attentions, it has never led to anything. I am quite sure you understand me."

Theodosia met her gaze coolly. "If you mean to tell me that your brother is a pleasant companion but that I ought not to have a *tendre* for him, I understand you very well. And I know you will not take it amiss if I give *you* a warning, Miss Cranley. In most circles it is not considered *comme il faut* to disparage one's relations to relative strangers."

For a moment matters hung in the balance, but Miss Cranley's rigid upbringing asserted itself and she said smoothly, "I shall ring for a tea tray, Lady Theodosia. I fear you have indulged a trifle too freely, and the tea will do you good."

Helena would have protested hotly in her friend's defense, but at that moment the gentlemen entered the room, having decided to forgo their brandy. Both the tea tray and Theodosia's defense were forgotten in the bustle as the colonel's chess set was brought out for his habitual game with Reverend Seeley.

Everyone else was left to chat together. Theodosia and Helena found themselves questioned closely about Bath by the Wartons. Meanwhile Holwell and Peter Cranley seized the opportunity to discuss the merits of various clubs in London. Perhaps that is why Theodosia did not notice Stanwood *tête-à-tête* with Clarissa. Indeed, she became aware of the situation only when Clarissa's high-pitched laugh rang out.

"Oh, Stanwood, how absurd!" she cried.

Helena's face darkened. "What is so absurd?" she muttered.

Helena did not have long to wait to find out. Clarissa rose and walked toward the group around Stanwood's sister, and her first words when she reached them were, "Hidden treasure! How like you to be excited about such nonsense, Helena. The notion that your grandfather had a fortune to hide is ridiculous."

"Fortune? Hidden?" Peter's eager voice asked.

Helena turned to him, grateful for a friendly face. "Cousin Roberta told us that's what Grandfather said. And we have found some of his journals and Bartram has the strongbox we found in the ruins in his room. With keys and directions for finding *'something'* given in code."

"Most unlikely," Holwell said judiciously, "and yet I think it is a harmless pursuit for Miss Stanwood and Lady Theodosia."

"Why, Sir Thomas, how generous of you!" Theodosia said, in a tone heavy with irony.

Pleased, he bowed. Stanwood resolutely turned the talk to another direction, suggesting Clarissa sing for them. It was a notion avidly seconded by Holwell, and Clarissa soon agreed. Peter Cranley excused himself, pleading a sudden need to attend to matters elsewhere. A short time later, Theodosia found herself wishing she might have done the same. Instead, to preserve them all from an encore already being requested, she volunteered to sing if Helena would accompany her on the pianoforte and someone would turn the pages of the music for Helena.

14

The party that rode back to Stanwood Oaks that evening was a grimly silent one. Helena was still smarting from the snubs Clarissa Cranley had administered. Theodosia seemed lost in her own thoughts, and Stanwood and Holwell regarded each other with wary disapproval.

"I did not see the need to take our leave quite so early from our hostess," Holwell said at last.

"Indeed. You seemed to quite enjoy her company," Stanwood replied crisply.

"Our hostess was Mrs. Cranley," Holwell said icily. "I collect, however, you mean to suggest that I enjoyed Miss Cranley's company. The answer to that is yes, I did," Holwell agreed. "Miss Cranley appears to be a most sensible and unexceptionable young woman. *Quite* a pleasant change from the young girls to be found in London and Bath."

"Such as Dosie and myself?" Helena asked innocently.

Bartram quelled her with a look. To Holwell he said shortly, "I don't doubt you found Miss Cranley sensible and pleasant company. Nevertheless I felt it best to be starting back. The roads are not of the best around here and even by moonlight not the easiest to traverse."

Holwell nodded, somewhat mollified. "True." He even relaxed so far as to smile and nod toward the two young women. "Your sister and Lady Theodosia will no doubt be grateful for their rest. It is easy to indulge a trifle too freely when one is not accustomed to wine."

Helena gasped. "What a bouncer!" she said, outraged. "I had no more than at home!"

"I think Sir Thomas refers to me," Theodosia interrupted her friend gently. "Or perhaps it was simply the gaiety of the evening that led me to forget my natural modesty and address everyone so freely. But after all, Clarissa did bid me to feel at home, as though I had known everyone all my life."

Holwell patted her hand and said soothingly, "True, true, my dear. It is your natural innocence and good nature that sometimes lead you astray, no doubt. I do not regard it and I am sure the others understood as well."

Not a trace of any emotion other than a smile crossed Theodosia's face, and yet Stanwood had the sudden urge to reach out and draw her to his side and defend her, saying that at least she showed spirit rather than an excess of civility that night. Unfortunately it occurred to him that to do so was to draw an unflattering comparison with the woman he expected to wed—Clarissa Cranley. So, instead, Stanwood turned the talk to other matters and the rest of the journey was accomplished in relative comfort.

When they reached the house, Holwell retired to his room, pleading fatigue. Stanwood said he preferred the library and Theodosia and Helena elected to go to a quiet sitting room where they could talk over the entire evening. They were still doing so sometime later when Stanwood's rough voice interrupted them.

Striding into the room, he said impatiently, "Nella! I wish to speak with you."

Puzzled, Helena asked, "What about, Bartram?"

He halted as he saw Theodosia, though he must have known she would be there. After a brief moment, however, he appeared to make up his mind. "What the devil have you done with the strongbox?" he demanded angrily.

"The strongbox?" Helena looked at him astounded.

"Don't pretend innocence," Stanwood told her harshly. "I know very well you must have taken it. No doubt to look over with Lady Theodosia. Where is it? Here on the sofa with you?"

"How dare you!" Helena began hotly.

Theodosia cut her short, however, by standing up between them. She pointed to the sofa and said, "Look for yourself. It isn't here."

Stanwood regarded Theodosia angrily. "Where is it, then?" he demanded.

Theodosia met his gaze squarely. "I don't know," she said. "As far as I know, we don't have it." Before Helena could protest, Theodosia turned and said to her, "Apparently the box is missing, Nella, so if you do have it, you'd best say so right now. Otherwise we had better think about where it might be. If someone else has taken it, however, then that is a matter I think we need to take seriously."

Sober now, Stanwood looked at his sister, who said quietly, "I don't have it. Truly, Dosie. But who does?"

Again Theodosia intervened. "Are you quite certain you could not have misplaced it?" she asked Stanwood.

He shook his head. "Quite certain."

"Moved by one of the servants?" Theodosia suggested.

Stanwood hesitated. "Perhaps," he conceded, "though I cannot think it likely."

With her usual good sense Theodosia replied, "In the morning, I think that the best place to begin. If it has not reappeared."

"But what if it was not moved by one of the servants?" Helena asked.

"Then," Theodosia said gravely, "we begin to ask who else might have taken it."

Stanwood nodded and was about to turn away, when Theodosia's voice halted him. "Was everything still in the box?" she asked.

He frowned. "No," he said frankly. "I had

taken out the keys and put them elsewhere."

"Where?" Helena demanded.

Theodosia held up a warning hand. "No, Nella, I don't think we want to know. But I would suggest, Lord Stanwood, that you make sure they are in a very safe place."

"I shall," he told her gravely.

Again Stanwood turned to go, and again Theodosia's voice halted him. There was a touch of wry humor to her voice as she said, "Do you think, perhaps, we are being a bit absurd about all this? Making a great deal out of some servant's careless action?"

Stanwood smiled at her reassuringly. "Let us hope so," he said. "And yet, if someone has taken it, this is a more serious matter than I had bargained for. Who can it be? You? Nella? Sir Thomas? Cousin Roberta? Or one of the servants? I cannot believe it of them. I should have sworn every one was loyal to the family. No, Lady Theodosia, I very much hope that you are correct and one of the servants moved it carelessly." Stanwood had reached the door by now, and he added, "I suggest you get some sleep. I intend to be up early to search for the box, and surely you will wish to join me!"

In answer, Helena threw an angry look at the rapidly closing door, then turned to Theodosia to speculate eagerly over what had occurred. "Who could have taken it?" she demanded. "Can you truly imagine Cousin Roberta stealing into Bartram's room and out again, a strongbox under her arm? Perhaps it was Holwell! Or some dis-

gruntled servant who, despite what Bartram
said, has taken the family in the greatest dislike.
Perhaps it is even an illegitimate son or daughter
of my Grandfather or father!"

"Nella," Theodosia began warningly, "I don't
think we ought to talk this way! What if one of
the servants should overhear us? You have far
too much imagination, but a servant might think
you were serious."

"Well, and so I am," Helena retorted
indignantly. "How could you think otherwise?
But tell me," she went on eagerly, "what are your
own thoughts upon the matter? Or would you
rather talk about Clarissa's brother, Peter?"

Eventually Theodosia found herself back in her
own room. She ought, she knew, to have been
turning her thoughts to the question of where the
box might be. Instead she found herself thinking
of Stanwood and how he had looked at dinner.
From there her thoughts drifted to the pleasant-
est of daydreams. Abruptly, however, Theodosia
pulled herself out of her reverie. More absurd
than all the rest was the notion that if Stanwood
were to develop a *tendre* for her, the match would
be allowed. No, Theodosia's mother was far too
ambitious, she knew, to allow her daughter to
marry a man without funds. Grandmama might
give her consent, but if word reached Mama, she
would be back in England as soon as the first ship
that crossed the Atlantic would allow. One could
elope, of course, or marry in haste, but that was
not the way an Elston would choose to wed.

For that matter, Theodosia asked herself

sharply, where was her resolve, her determination
never to give up her freedom? Was this foolish
attraction to Stanwood to outweigh all her
principles? Abruptly Theodosia felt her head
throb with what she knew to be the start of an
unenviable headache. Sighing, she finished
brushing out her hair and sought her bed.

15

Stanwood came awake abruptly, roused by something he could not name. Quietly he lay there, his breathing still regular, listening. Near him came the sound of someone else's breathing, and a moment later the viscount felt a hand reach under his pillow. Immediately his own hand shot out and he grabbed for the invader. There was a struggle and something heavy crashed down on Stanwood's head. The last thing he knew, he was falling out of bed.

16

Humming slightly to herself, Theodosia arranged the flowers cut for her by Humphrey in the dining room. Up since dawn, she had had time to attend to a few domestic matters before anyone was about. Not that it was her place to do so, Theodosia reminded herself with a sigh, but who else could? Mrs. Thompson, the house-keeper, had been laid low with a toothache and had gratefully seized on Theodosia for help. Helena had no notion how to run a household and did not wish to try, and Cousin Roberta's efforts resulted in more trouble than anything else. Nor did she seem to mind that Theodosia had taken over the reins.

For a moment Theodosia paused and considered the odd woman the Stanwoods had placed in charge of their daughter. At one time, the late viscount's Cousin Roberta must have been a beauty. Why, then, had she never married? Theodosia wondered. Time had changed that beauty to something that in another woman might have appeared distinguished. With Cousin Roberta, however, one only found oneself wanting to pity her. Nor was that an emotion Miss Stanwood tried to discourage.

Would she herself be like that one day? Theodosia wondered. Her independence turned to querulousness? Her pride turned to moments of absurdly useless arrogance? Her mind dulled by the want of challenging conversation so that in time it seemed to wander and no one, in any event, ever took her seriously? It was not a pleasant thought.

As Theodosia stood there thinking, a servant rushed into the room, his face alternately pale and then very red. "Lady Theodosia!" he cried as soon as he saw her. "There's been . . . that is . . . this is most improper, but none of the family are up and about . . ."

"*Who* are you?" Theodosia asked with creditable calm.

"Lord Stanwood's valet," the fellow answered in a rush. "It's his lordship; he's hurt. Bashed over the head, I'd say. But how could such a thing happen *here*?"

At the valet's words Theodosia had dropped the flowers in her hand and gone quite pale. Her voice was scarcely above a whisper as she said, "When? Where? Is he . . . is he . . . ?"

Her voice trailed off and the valet hastened to reassure her. "No, no, he's unconscious but not dead. Yet. I've already sent for the doctor, but someone ought to see to him now!"

"Yes, yes, of course," Theodosia said, collecting herself. "I'll come straightaway. Have you any smelling salts?"

"The cook is looking for hers," the valet explained. "But what about the family? Ought we to rouse them?"

Theodosia hesitated, then shook her head decisively. "No. Not until we know how matters stand. Miss Stanwood might become hysterical and Helena will worry needlessly."

"Might not be needlessly," the valet muttered darkly. "You ain't seen the wound."

The words were not reassuring, but Theodosia forced herself to be calm as they mounted the stairs and she asked for an account of what had occurred. "Don't know, your ladyship," the valet replied earnestly. "I went to rouse his lordship, as usual, and there he was—on the floor. Out cold, too. Looked as if he'd been there some time. And hit on the back of the head by something heavy. Dunno what."

"I see," Theodosia said, trying to sound in command. "Is he still on the floor?"

"Of course not!" the valet was shocked at such a notion.

Theodosia nodded but persisted. "And was he dressed when you found him?"

"Only in his nightshirt. Found him right on the floor beside the bed. You'd think he just fell out if you didn't see the bump on his head."

Theodosia's hand gripped the balustrade tighter and she fell silent until they reached the viscount's room. Then she was unable to suppress a gasp as she saw how pale he looked lying on his bed in the strong morning sunlight. Swiftly she moved to his side and felt his wrist. The steady pulse there calmed her somewhat, and just then a knock sounded briefly at the door as the cook entered with her vinaigrette.

With a slight curtsy she held it out to Theodosia and said, "The smelling salts, m'lady." Coming closer, she looked at the viscount and shuddered. "Dear Lord, it'll be a miracle if he lives!"

Resolutely Theodosia squared her shoulders and spoke in a tone of deliberate coolness. "He shall. His condition looks far worse than it is. If you could go to the kitchen, however, and make some strengthening broth, Mrs. Wren . . . "

"Of course, at once, m'lady," the cook said, curtsying again as she backed to the door.

The valet had also brightened at Theodosia's words, and she could only hope they would prove justified. Panic, however, could not help the household, and she had at least held that at bay. With a scarcely suppressed sigh, Theodosia turned to her patient and gently waved the smelling salts beneath the viscount's nose. After a few seconds he began to move and lose a little of his pallor. Angrily he began to mutter, but he still did not seem to know her. Alarmed, Theodosia turned to speak to the valet, but he was already greeting the doctor at the bedroom door. Startled, she said, "How did you arrive so quickly?"

The doctor looked surprised. "I was just

leaving a nearby household when Stanwood's groom found me. Who are you to be asking?"

Swiftly Theodosia collected herself and held out a hand in greeting. "I am Lady Theodosia Elston. A houseguest of Lord Stanwood's. None of the family were up and about when his lordship's valet found him, so they came to me for help. I've managed to rouse him with smelling salts, but he doesn't seem quite . . . quite himself."

"Delirious?" the doctor asked with a nod. "Well, let me take a look at him. If you'll wait outside, please?"

Hastily Theodosia did as she was bid. She was hard pressed, however, to wait patiently, and found herself pacing back and forth outside the viscount's door. As she waited, Helena arrived, and it was evident she had dressed quickly.

A trifle breathless, she said, "Dosie, what happened? Clara told me Bartram was hurt, perhaps even dead."

With an effort Theodosia forced herself to speak calmly. "He is hurt. But the doctor is with him now."

"But what happened?" Helena persisted.

"I don't know. It looks, however, as though someone struck him over the head."

"The journals!" Helena said, her voice scarcely above a whisper.

"More likely the keys," Theodosia retorted tartly, "unless it was just an ordinary thief."

"Is anything else missing?" Helena demanded.

"I don't know," Theodosia admitted

reluctantly. "I didn't think to ask, but I suppose one of the servants would have said if there had been anything obvious of value missing."

"Well, we shall have the servants institute a search as soon as we hear how Bartram is doing," Helena said briskly, "and that had better be soon!"

Just then the doctor came out of the room and looked from Theodosia to Helena. "How is my brother?" Helena demanded.

The doctor sighed. "He has taken no permanent injury, I believe. But it is important that he should have careful nursing. On no account is he to leave his bed before I give permission, nor is he to be distressed by persons hovering over him and fluttering nervously."

Helena drew herself up in anger and was about to retort that there was no one who fluttered nervously here when she saw Cousin Roberta coming toward them. The doctor also saw her and turned to greet her. "Oh, doctor," she said, trembling, "is it true? Is the viscount dead?"

Soothingly he said, "No, he has merely injured himself in a fall. His manservant has matters well in hand and I have given him the necessary instructions. Now, who is in charge of the still-room here?" he concluded briskly.

For a moment no one answered and then Theodosia said quietly, "I am." The doctor looked at her with raised eyebrows and she went on defensively, "I am only a guest in this household; however, I have a great deal of experience in the stillroom at home, and the viscount gave me per-

mission to try my hand at restocking his, for it is
sadly depleted."

"Dosie's a great hand at domestic matters,"
Helena added proudly.

"Oh, my, yes, Lady Theodosia has been *most*
helpful," Cousin Roberta agreed immediately.

"Very well, you seem a sensible young lady,"
the doctor said at last. "If there is somewhere we
may consult, I shall advise you which preparations are likely to help his lordship the most."

"Of course, doctor, this way," Theodosia said,
leading him to the former Lady Stanwood's
sitting room on that floor. As she walked she
explained, "Unfortunately, the supplies are sadly
depleted; nevertheless, I do not despair that we
may find something useful there. Or send for it
from another household."

The doctor nodded, but when they reached the
sitting room it turned out the doctor had other
matters on his mind. "I have already spoken to
the manservant," he said curtly, "and he has
given me some notion what supplies you have on
hand. You may consult with him when I have left.
In your hands and his I leave the nursing, and as
I said before, no one is to be forever fussing about
him, nor is he to be let up before I give my permission."

Theodosia faced him squarely. "I see. May I
ask, then, why you wished to speak with me?"

"Because, young as you are, you appear to be
the most sensible person here. The manservant
had already told me you were in and out of the
stillroom since your arrival, and it seemed the

least obvious way to arrange to speak with you alone. And I did wish to speak with someone alone, someone who will *not* become hysterical at what I have to say. Had his lordship any enemies?''

"I . . . I don't know," Theodosia answered frankly. "I cannot think it likely, and in any event, could it not have been an ordinary thief?"

The doctor gave her a long, level look. "So you know he was attacked?"

"His valet told me. And showed me the wound. He could not have struck his head in that manner simply by falling out of bed," Theodosia replied evenly.

"You are quite correct," the doctor said as he nodded. "And perhaps it was an ordinary thief. The servants, however, insist nothing has been taken, nor any windows forced, but that does not mean no one entered—it simply means that whoever entered probably knew his way about."

"It appears the servants were quite busy before they notified anyone," Theodosia said dryly.

Again the doctor nodded. "They were, let us say, careful. I understand you were the only one awake and they were understandably reluctant to approach a guest with what ought to be family business. That they did so at all is part of what has convinced me to place his lordship's care in your hands."

"Thank you," Theodosia said quietly. "And I wish I could tell you who might have done this, but I cannot."

"Well, keep your eyes and wits about you and we shall speak further when I check my patient later," the doctor said briskly. "Now, if you will show me out . . ."

Theodosia did so, and his last words to her were, "Good luck, Lady Theodosia. I do not think you will find his lordship an easy patient."

Theodosia laughed. "That, sir, I do not doubt!"

17

Theodosia's first action was to go back and look in on Lord Stanwood. Or rather, she tried to. Stanwood's valet answered her soft knock at the door and informed her that he was helping his lordship attend to his needs and that it would be better if her ladyship returned later. He then repeated some of the doctor's requests for supplies from the stillroom. Thus neatly snubbed, Theodosia nodded and decided to join whoever might be in the breakfast room. It would be best to see what was being said and allay any fears.

As she entered the breakfast room, Theodosia noted that everyone was already there. Cousin Roberta was, as might be expected, all aflutter, Helena looked as if she might cry at any moment, and even Holwell looked as though he had slept badly. Theodosia was touched by the concern etched upon his face.

"Good morning," Theodosia said, resolutely cheerful. "The doctor says that Lord Stanwood will recover nicely and that we must simply see that he rests for a day or two until the doctor feels it safe for him to leave his bed."

"What, er, happened?" Holwell asked delicately.

"He has hurt himself," Cousin Roberta sobbed into her large handkerchief. "And I must, simply must, nurse him. I should never forgive myself if I did not!"

Tactfully Theodosia replied, "Why, Miss Stanwood, you must not!" As that lady looked at her in astonishment, Theodosia went on, "The doctor is most concerned that you do not lose your strength. His lordship's man will look after him for the most part, and even I am relegated to the role of dispensing cordials and such from the still-room. Men prefer their own company at such times, I believe."

"*I* should never refuse yours," Holwell said, gazing at Theodosia soulfully. Then, as if recollecting himself, he said briskly, "But what did happen?"

"His lordship appears to have had a fall and hurt his head," Theodosia said, looking away as she pretended an interest in her teacup.

"Fell and hurt himself?" Helena demanded indignantly. "You know very well he was struck, Dosie!"

With a sigh, Theodosia met her friend's eyes. Coming to a rapid decision, she said, "Very true, it appears he was struck upon the head. I had hoped, however, to avoid alarming Miss

Stanwood or Sir Thomas by saying so. Since you have, let me repeat that Lord Stanwood will recover and that the servants are under orders to see that no entrances are left unbarred tonight."

"Then you think it a common housebreaker?" Holwell asked. "Should we not notify the nearest magistrate?"

"I knew it! I knew it!" Cousin Roberta's voice broke in before Theodosia was forced to answer. "I could not sleep last night and I heard noises. I knew there was someone about! I even went so far as to light my candle and look in the corridor, did I not, Sir Thomas? We both heard something, did we not, Sir Thomas?"

As Theodosia and Helena turned to him in surprise, Holwell colored deeply. "I . . . I had difficulty sleeping and did encounter Miss Stanwood in the corridor. And . . . and perhaps I did hear a sound, but I did not . . . did not take it as a matter of concern."

Helena gave Theodosia a long, hard look, but before either could speak, a voice was heard approaching the room. A moment later Peter Cranley stood in the doorway greeting them. "I say, how is Stanwood? Recovered yet from the bump on the head?"

It was Holwell who handled matters. Drawing himself up to standing, Sir Thomas said in a voice that might have frozen a lesser fellow, "I think, Mr. Cranley, that you owe us an explanation. How do you know that Lord Stanwood was struck on the head?"

Cranley blinked. "Struck on the head?" he repeated. "I thought he just fell out of bed or something."

"I repeat, Mr. Cranley, how do you know of Lord Stanwood's injury?" Holwell persisted impassively.

"Mrs. Thompson told me." Peter Cranley shrugged as he threw himself into the nearest chair and reached for a roll from one of those on the table. "Her daughter works for us, and I stopped round back to pass on a message. And she told me."

"Her *daughter*?" Holwell asked, eyebrows raised. "Ought I to ask your connection with the daughter?"

Cranley set down the roll and frowned. "You are a dashed impertinent fellow, Sir Thomas," he said. "But I shan't regard it. I do wish, however, that someone would tell me what was going on here. You said Stanwood was struck on the head?"

Theodosia weighed matters but spoke quickly to forestall Helena's impetuous reply. "A thief, perhaps. In any event, the matter is best forgotten. The servants are taking measures to ensure that future thieves will find the task of breaking in far more difficult." Theodosia had spoken with a lightness she did not feel, and now she avoided Helena's eyes. Instead she turned to Cranley and said amiably, "Did you come only to pass on a message to Mrs. Thompson, or did you come to see us as well?"

"Oh, to see you as well," he said gallantly.

"And ask if you and Helena would like to go out riding with me. Oh, and Sir Thomas, if he cares to, as well."

With scarcely suppressed distaste Holwell replied, "I most certainly would. I must consider it my duty, while his lordship is incapacitated, to look after the ladies."

"Ought we to leave Bartram?" Helena asked anxiously.

"I shall not," Theodosia said decisively, "but you will. There are matters in the stillroom I must attend to, but you are to go out riding, Nella, and try to forget this. Your brother will be quite himself in a trice, and there is no need to forgo your pleasure now. Nor you, Sir Thomas. I insist you all go out riding and enjoy yourselves."

Holwell, who had been about to object, had no choice but to bow graciously and go upstairs to change his clothes. Theodosia then turned to Helena and said calmly, "Come, Nella, I shall help you with your things. I am sure Mr. Cranley will excuse us."

Peter Cranley graciously nodded, and the two young women left the room. Only Cousin Roberta remained, and Peter Cranley found it no trouble to give soothing replies to her anxious utterances.

Sometime later Theodosia emerged from the stillroom, a basket over her arm filled with assorted labeled bottles. Behind her wafted the smell of potions in the process of being distilled or simmered. She then made a brief stop in the kitchens, which produced a tray to be carried upstairs by a maid following directly behind Theodosia.

Rather satisfied with her efforts, Theodosia mounted the stairs and rapped on his lordship's door.

"Come in!" was the snarled reply.

Immediately that was followed by a familiar, rather timid voice saying, "Oh, but I really *don't* think visitors would be wise!"

Firmly Theodosia pushed open the door and beckoned the maid to follow her. Speaking a trifle curtly she said, "Where is your valet, my lord?"

Cousin Roberta answered for Stanwood. "Oh dear, an errand called him away and I just felt that his lordship ought *not* be left alone!"

"And I keep telling you that is just what I should prefer!" Stanwood retorted shortly.

"Dear, dear, such a temper. A nap would do you so much good, I know," Roberta replied, making an ineffectual attempt to plump Stanwood's pillow.

As the viscount's color rose, Theodosia hastily intervened. "Miss Stanwood, could you be a dear and look over the drawing room for me? I fear we shall have callers as word of his lordship's injury gets about, and I just *cannot* get the flowers to look right."

Immediately Cousin Roberta brightened. "Why, of course, my dear, I should be delighted to be of assistance," she fluttered. "It does require a knack, I know. My mother was always used to say that the arrangement of flowers was one of my greatest talents!"

"I don't doubt it!" Stanwood said under his breath.

Cousin Roberta, however, heard him. With a distinct sniff she said, "Have your fun with me—I should not expect a man to understand."

Then, with head held high, she left the room.

"Flowers?" Stanwood demanded quizzically.

Theodosia gave a warning shake of her head as she directed the maid where to set down the tray of food. Her own basket was set to the side, where it would be handy for Lord Stanwood's valet to find. When the maid was gone, she said, "How are you feeling?"

"I've the devil of a headache—how do you think I should feel?" Stanwood demanded crossly. "Not helped by the presence of that meddling old biddy my cousin!"

Theodosia waited a moment before she answered him. Carefully she said, "Your cousin may have a point, however. It might be wise if you were not left alone."

"What the devil do you mean by that?" Stanwood demanded.

Again Theodosia spoke carefully. "The doctor feels, and your man and I agree, that you did not hurt your head yourself. That someone dealt you a blow. Whether housebreaker or not, I shall not be easy as to the possibility of the person's return to your rooms. Your man says that he believes nothing was taken, and so there might be reason for a return. Do you know who struck you?"

Standwood started to shake his head then cursed at the pain. Bitterly he replied, "No. I

remember nothing of what occurred. Not un-
common with such an injury, the doctor told
Henry, my valet. And I, too, suspect the person
may return. But I will not have Cousin Roberta
sitting with me! If it must be anyone, let it be
you! At least you are capable of sensible conversation."

For a moment Theodosia could not answer;
then, with creditable calm she replied, "Very well,
I shall arrange with . . . with Henry that either he
or I shall be with you at all times. For now I think
you should try to eat, though only a little, at
first."

To her surprise, the viscount meekly agreed
and even allowed her to help him when the spoon
shook unexpectedly. "A nearer case to death than
I had suspected, it seems," Stanwood joked
grimly.

"I cannot think it a matter for laughter,"
Theodosia replied curtly.

"No?" Stanwood asked, taking her hand in his.
"And here I thought you rather disliked me,
thinking me a tyrant over my poor sister—your
best friend."

Theodosia could not bring herself to meet his
gaze. "No, I . . . I have never disliked you," she
said at last, a trifle breathlessly.

"Not even before you met me?" he chided her
gently, still holding tightly to her hand.
Theodosia did not reply, and he went on, "Do you
know, Lady Theodosia, I think of you sometimes
as my charming impostor."

Alarmed, Theodosia's eyes flew to meet his.

What she saw there did nothing to reassure her or still her wildly beating heart. "Wh-whatever c-can you mean?" she stammered.

Oblivious of the tray on his lap, Stanwood reached out to draw Theodosia closer, something she found herself powerless to resist. "I don't know who you are," he said gravely. "When I first met you, you seemed such a sober young woman, years older than your age. Then, in my carriage coming here, a surprisingly fashionable young lady. Then, with Helena, a delightfully heedless child. And now . . . now—"

Before Stanwood could tell her more, the door opened and an anxious valet bustled into the room. Instantly Theodosia was on her feet, turning her back to the fellow to hide her crimson face as she busied herself with the tray. Over her shoulder she told him, "You'll find the cordials and such that Dr. Barnwood requested on the table."

"Very good, m'lady," he replied.

Mischievously Stanwood said heartily, "Henry, Lady Theodosia and I have decided that for the sake of my safety, I am never to be left alone. You and she shall share the onerous duty of keeping by my side."

"Now, now, your lordship, you shouldn't ought to joke about things like that," the valet answered heavily. "As for her ladyship, I don't see that as fitting. Perhaps one of the others—"

"No," Stanwood retorted decisively, "Lady Theodosia it must and shall be." Henry continued to regard him with sharp disapproval, and the viscount went on coaxingly, "Come, come, Henry, surely the doctor told you to humor me? Think of it, man! Can you see my sister behaving sensibly enough to do the task? Or my father's cousin, Miss Roberta Stanwood?"

Reluctantly Henry shook his head. "Very well," he said at last, "but I needn't like it. And what Miss Cranley will say is beyond me."

"Miss Cranley needn't know," Stanwood replied curtly. "In fact, with luck, she shan't hear of my injury at all until I'm better."

"Oh, but she shall," Theodosia warned him.

"How?"

"Peter was here early this morning and had already heard. From Mrs. Thompson, I believe he said," Theodosia replied expressionlessly. "I don't suppose he is familiar with how to enter the house at night?" she added cautiously.

For a moment Stanwood looked at her blankly; then with a harsh laugh he said, "Is that how it is, then? We are to suspect everyone near us? Why not Cousin Roberta? She has been here since we began searching for my grandfather's nonexistent legacy. *She* believes in it. Or your friend Holwell? He was here."

Theodosia was quiet a moment. Reluctantly she said, "Yes, and he was even seen wandering about the halls last night. Nevertheless, I cannot think it of him. No, we are surely indulging in foolish speculation."

Henry cut in to say, "P'rhaps, but someone bashed his lordship in the head."

"Accurately if indelicately put," Stanwood said

with a laugh. "Come, Lady Theodosia, forgo play-ing the part of Bow Street Runner! Your job is merely to see to it that I recover from this assault and to stay by my side until I do so. Then we shall worry about who was at fault. Agreed?"

He smiled at her so charmingly that in spite of herself Theodosia nodded. "Good girl," Stanwood told her heartily. "Now, off with you for a half-hour or so. Then come back and sit with me."

When she was gone, Henry turned to the viscount and said, "Is that really what you are thinking, your lordship?"

Stanwood gave him a withering look. "My wits have *not* gone begging, Henry. Now, here is what I want you to do when Lady Theodosia returns and you are free to leave me . . ."

18

It seemed to Theodosia that the half-hour until she could return to Lord Stanwood's room was an extraordinarily long one. The tasks that occupied her in the stillroom were not so demanding as to keep her mind from worrying about his lordship's condition. But she had expected that. What she did not expect was that she would arrive to discover that his lordship was asleep and that her time spent there would stretch on so long. Indeed, by the time Henry reappeared to take her place, Theodosia had begun to fear that something was amiss. "He is sleeping so soundly," she told the valet, a quiver of worry to her voice.

"Ah, that would be right." Henry nodded wisely. "His lordship is a hard man to keep quiet, and the doctor left a sleeping draft to help. He'll be coming round soon now, and not in the best of tempers."

Henry looked at the door and Theodosia reluctantly moved in that direction. "You will summon me if he takes a turn for the worse?" she asked anxiously.

"To be sure, m'lady," the fellow replied. "And now you'd best hurry if you don't wish to be late for tea."

Startled, Theodosia asked, "Is it that late already?"

"It is," Henry confirmed. "You've got no more than a quarter of an hour to freshen up a bit."

That settled the matter. Theodosia wished no gossip as to the amount of time she was spending in the sickroom. And there would be gossip if she were not down for tea. Theodosia had no doubt that word of his lordship's injury would have drawn callers. Miss Clarissa Cranley, if no others.

She was not mistaken. Miss Cranley was deep in conversation with Sir Thomas when Theodosia entered the room. As were Nella and Peter Cranley. Only Miss Roberta Stanwood held herself aloof, and that was no more than usual for her. At the sound of her footsteps, everyone turned anxious eyes on Theodosia and waited for her to speak.

With a lightness she did not feel, Theodosia said, "Lord Stanwood is recovering slowly but well, and we need have no fear on his account."

"May I see him?" Clarissa demanded. "I must see him."

Theodosia moved toward her and said sympathetically, "I'm sorry. The doctor has given orders that there are to be no visitors to his room just yet."

"But surely—" she began.

"No visitors," Theodosia repeated firmly.

"Yet you go there!" Clarissa retorted angrily.

Hastily Holwell intervened. "The doctor appointed Lady Theodosia to oversee his lordship's treatment. It is she, I do not doubt, who must deal with his lordship's anger over the doctor's orders. I, for one, do not envy her." Miss Cranley managed a wan smile and Holwell went on, "Please sit down, Miss Cranley. You have had a most dreadful shock, and while I do not doubt his lordship will soon recover, it is nevertheless a distress to you. I give you my word you shall be told as soon as he may have visitors."

Indeed? Theodosia thought. She did not speak, however, aloud.

Peter Cranley did. "Has the old boy come to yet? Can he tell us what occurred?"

All eyes were suddenly alertly fixed on Theodosia's face as she said quietly, "I'm afraid not. He can remember nothing after retiring for the night. And the doctor says that even if there were something to remember, it is quite likely he will never do so."

To Theodosia's taut nerves it seemed as though someone had sighed with relief at these words. But she could not have said who it was. At that moment Cousin Roberta's voice intruded. "Nella, will you please pass this cup of tea to Miss Cranley? And the next one to Lady Theodosia?"

Peter Cranley hastened to help, and soon talk had passed to lighter matters. Peter and Nella were deep in an argrument over the relative merits of two horses in his stable, and Clarissa and Holwell were discussing old friends they suddenly discovered they shared. Theodosia was thus left to the company of Miss Roberta Stanwood, who said in a troubled voice, "I blame myself for all this, Lady Theodosia."

"Whatever can you mean?" Theodosia asked in genuine astonishment.

"Well, if I had never brought up the tale of the treasure . . ." Her voice drifted off for a moment; then Roberta resolutely pursued the point. "Of course, I am sure his lordship's injury has nothing to do with the matter but had I not repeated that absurd tale, Peter Cranley would doubtless not be so interested in being here, and your gentleman would not be hanging so on Miss Cranley's words."

Tactfully Theodosia replied, "We do not yet know that the tale was an absurd one. Indeed, all evidence points the other way. As to the rest, you are too harsh with yourself. Surely Peter Cranley cannot care about the matter, and Sir Thomas would have stayed on in any event. As for his interest in Miss Cranley, that cannot be laid at anyone's door save his own. And mine, perhaps, for not being a more fascinating companion."

Miss Stanwood hesitated, then said, "Yes, but Peter Cranley does care! He said so in the breakfast room when the rest of you had left. He . . . he seemed *passionately* concerned. I did my best, of course, to tell him it was a silly tale, no more, but he would not be convinced. He fears, I think, that his father means to cut him off without a feather

to fly with. And . . . and I fear he lied when he said
he learned of my cousin's injury from Mrs.
Thompson. I do not like to carry tales, but I
would swear I saw him here last night. As for Sir
Thomas, well, again, I do not like to carry tales,
but . . . but there has been bad blood between his
family and the Stanwoods. There are times when
I swear I see vengeance in his eyes." She hesitated again and then said, "I know you will think
me a foolish old woman, but please see that his
lordship is not ever left alone. I . . . I cannot be
easy about him. Even I, though I am not a strong
woman, might be of some protection to him."

Theodosia patted her hand reassuringly. "I
have already taken steps to see to the matter.
Either I or Lord Stanwood's valet will be on hand
at all times. As for the other matters, well, we
must wait and see."

Miss Stanwood nodded, her eyes misting
slightly. "What a wise young woman you are,"
she said approvingly.

There was nothing one could say to that, and
Theodosia was relieved when Peter Cranley
claimed her attention. Drawing her to a far corner
of the room, he asked her seriously, "How is he
really? Stanwood, I mean."

"As well as can be expected," Theodosia said
lightly. "Someone is always with him, and I
expect his lordship to be himself again in a few
days."

"And the treasure?" Peter asked quickly.

Theodosia hesitated. Looking down at her

hands, she said, "I'm afraid that is a matter none of us has time for until his lordship is on his feet again."

Cranley might have protested, but at that moment Holwell cleared his throat behind him. "My dear Lady Theodosia," he said in a kindly voice, "do you think such a *tête-à-tête* wise? You must have a care for your reputation, you know."

Coolly Theodosia replied, "Indeed? And who here do you think likely to carry tales?"

"Why . . . why, no one," Holwell sputtered, taken aback. "I simply meant that one should . . . should always consider the appearance of one's behavior."

"Indeed, I agree," Theodosia said quietly, "and that is why I suggest that you refrain from wandering the halls at night."

"Good God, Lady Theodosia, are you questioning my conduct?" Holwell asked in surprise. "I had not thought it possible. Whatever can you accuse me of?"

"I should think it obvious," Peter Cranley said coolly. "With Stanwood ill because someone bashed him on the head, Lady Theodosia's right when she says such wanderings might give people odd notions of you."

The two men might have come to blows had Clarissa Cranley not broken in by saying, "Peter, you've no right to speak to Sir Thomas in such a way. Why, look to your own behavior! Was it right to excuse yourself and desert the dinner party last night?"

"Yes, and Cousin Roberta says she saw you prowling around here last night!" Helena exclaimed excitedly.

Theodosia frowned at her friend, but Nella ignored her. Peter Cranley's color rose and he stammered hotly, "Sh-she couldn't have!"

"Oh, no?" Holwell asked. "Do you question the lady's veracity?"

"No, only her eyesight," Peter retorted.

"Indeed? And will you question mine when I say that I saw you also?" Holwell demanded cruelly.

Peter looked around at the faces and finally said, "There's no point in defending myself, is there? You've all of you made up your minds, and that's the way it always is!"

And with that he flung himself out of the room. Behind him Theodosia bit her lower lip and Holwell and Clarissa exchanged looks of disapproval. Sir Thomas, in fact, moved closer to Miss Cranley and said sympathetically, "It must be difficult for you, with such a rapscallion for a brother."

As the two moved away to the far side of the room, Nella and Dosia heard her reply, "Yes, our mother has never been able to take a strong hand with him, and so it has fallen to me to try to raise him."

"Raise him, indeed!" Nella snorted. "More likely ruin him. No matter what anyone says, I won't believe there's more than mere mischief to Peter."

"But you're the one who challenged him," Theodosia pointed out curiously.

"I know," Helena agreed reluctantly, "but I only wanted to know if it was true. That he'd been here last night. But he couldn't have attacked Bartram, could he?"

"I don't know," Theodosia said quietly. "I don't know. It all seems mad, no matter whom we accuse. Unless we decide it was some unknown outsider. But I cannot credit it. Nothing was taken, and to say that your brother was attacked by mere coincidence just after the strongbox was taken is doing it much too brown."

"Where is the strongbox?" Helena asked curiously. "Did you see it in Bartram's room?"

Theodosia laughed wryly. "Do you know, with all this madness, I had completely forgotten to look? I suppose I had best ask Henry when I go upstairs again. But what shall we do about Peter Cranley?"

A trifle defiantly Helena said, "You needn't do anything. I'm going to go after him!"

Theodosia watched her friend leave and, with a sigh, turned back to the guests. Somehow she managed to muddle through the next half-hour, and then Miss Cranley took her leave. Sir Thomas graciously offered to escort her to the door, and Miss Cranley agreed, tossing Theodosia a look that might almost have been triumph.

A moment later Miss Roberta Stanwood excused herself for some vague reason and Theodosia was free to go upstairs to his lordship's room. This time she hoped he would be awake. In spite of his valet's words, Theodosia was still not easy in her mind about his condition.

19

His lordship was indeed awake. "Hello, Lady Theodosia," he greeted her as she entered his room. "Are you the one I have to thank for this absurd gruel I am allowed for my meals?"

Henry, the valet, stood respectfully at Stanwood's bedside and gave her a commiserating look. Briskly Theodosia advanced to the bed and replied, "No, you may thank the cook for that. And the doctor for his orders. I realize it must be a trying situation for you, but by tomorrow, *if* you appear much improved, we are to allow you a more normal diet."

"Then I shall assuredly be much improved tomorrow!" the viscount said with emphasis.

Theodosia did not miss, however, the fact that he then closed his eyes as though tired. Quietly she said to the valet, "I shall look after him for a while."

Henry nodded correctly and then withdrew. When he was gone, Theodosia seated herself beside Stanwood's bed. Immediately Stanwood's hand shot out and grasped Theodosia's wrist. Unperturbed, she made no effort to free herself. "It's my charming impostor again," he said with a grimace. "And what part did you play downstairs just now? The delightful hostess? It is a part I do not doubt you play to perfection."

Whereas there had been gentle amusement before when the viscount called her a "charming impostor," Theodosia now heard only anger. With a calm she did not feel she said, "May I ask how I have offended you, my lord?"

Stanwood's eyes met hers, and again Theodosia could read only anger there. "Why did you come here?" he demanded. "Because my cousin spread her tales about a treasure even in Bath?" In spite of herself, Theodosia gasped. Stanwood ignored her and went on, "And Sir Thomas? Is this the way he evens the score with my family?" Stanwood turned his face away from her but did not let go her wrist as he went on, "No doubt you did not expect it, but my man slipped out long enough to search the bedrooms while you were at tea. *All* the rooms. And in yours and in Holwell's he found . . . evidence."

At last Theodosia found her tongue. Incredulously she demanded, "Evidence? What evidence?"

Again Stanwood met her eyes. Very deliberately he said, "In Holwell's room he found a statue that might have been used to club me. In yours, under your bed, he found the strongbox."

"That cannot be!" Theodosia protested, her

face very pale. "I swear I did not put it there!"

With astonishing strength Stanwood pulled on Theodosia's wrist until she found herself bending over the bed. "No?" he demanded cruelly. "Where did you put it? I thought I had at last met a woman I could admire and respect and . . . and far more. But you have proved to me I was much mistaken. I can guess what your plans were, but you were so foolish! You might have had much more, including my title and home, as well as the treasure, for I was mad enough to believe myself falling in love with you!"

And before Theodosia could protest or even guess what he was about, Stanwood had pulled her down and held her tight with both arms while his lips closed over hers punishingly. In all her sheltered life Theodosia had never been kissed as Stanwood now kissed her, nor ever wanted to be kissed in such a way. But as he held her in his crushing grip, she found herself growing light-headed with desire for more of the same. In spite of all her upbringing, in spite of her knowledge of the impropriety, Theodosia found herself responding, wanting more, and reaching for it. It was only Cousin Roberta's shocked voice that brought her back to reality.

"*Lady Theodosia!*" Miss Stanwood exclaimed. "Please stop! You must stop!"

Before Roberta's voice had even died away, Theodosia was on her feet, hands trembling, desperately trying to smooth her skirt. She tried to speak but could not, and with a cry flung herself out of the room. Behind her she could hear Miss

Stanwood remonstrating with the viscount, and then Henry's soothing voice hastening the lady out of the room. Anxious, above all, to avoid Miss Stanwood and the scold that would surely ensue, Theodosia picked up her skirts and ran for the stairs at the end of the hall. Somehow she must find a deserted room to hide in while she tried to make sense of what had occurred.

She found her deserted room and, safely ensconced there, gave vent to all her tears. An hour and a half later she was no closer to a solution, only resolved to leave for Bath in the morning. She could not, would not, remain at Stanwood Oaks another day.

Helena, however, to whom Theodosia confided her resolve, was indignant. "You cannot leave, Dosie! Who will help me look after Bartram? Yes, yes, I know he has some absurd notion in his head that you and Holwell attacked him, but that is only because he does not know you as I do. Perhaps his wits are even addled. All the more reason to stay and discover who *is* after him. Would you leave my brother unprotected? Henry and I cannot do all the nursing ourselves. Indeed, I cannot do any at all, beyond fluffing pillows and the like."

Reluctantly Theodosia allowed herself to be persuaded to remain. "But I will not enter your brother's room again," she warned Helena forthrightly.

Nevertheless, that very evening Theodosia found herself doing so. The doctor had arrived and told her to accompany him to the sickroom.

"For I'd just as soon there were two of you knew how to change his lordship's dressing, and I don't know whom else I'd trust here," the doctor told Theodosia bluntly.

So, silently, she followed him. Entering the room, she met Stanwood's eyes briefly, and it seemed to her there was no lessening of the anger she had seen there before. Without a word, he tolerated the doctor's ministrations and allowed both Henry and Theodosia to replace the bandages about his head. Even Henry was more reserved than ever.

When the doctor was finished, Theodosia started to leave the room with him, but Stanwood's voice halted her. "Lady Theodosia, please be so good as to remain," he said.

Theodosia looked at the doctor questioningly. He nodded and said, "I shall speak to the family, but I think you know everything that needs to be done."

Keeping a careful distance from the bed, Theodosia waited until the doctor had closed the door behind him, and then she said, her voice surprisingly steady, "What is it you wish to say, Lord Stanwood?"

Grimly he answered her, "My sister tells me you are to remain. At her request. To nurse me. The doctor concurs. Very well. But I warn you, Lady Theodosia, my man will be watching for trouble, and next time you shan't get away uncaught." Theodosia did not choose to answer, and after a moment he went on, "What? No reply? A pity. Will you tell me, at least, how work

progresses on deciphering the code my grandfather left? Do you think you know yet where the
treasure is to be found? That was my first
thought, you know, when Nella told me you were
planning to leave. Either that you had cried
craven or that you had already found the treasure
and meant to take it with you."

Without a word Theodosia turned on her heel
and left the room. Behind her she could hear the
viscount's curse as a pillow was flung after her.

20

At breakfast the next morning Theodosia found everyone except herself in excellent spirits. Helena seemed positively to bubble with suppressed excitement, and even Miss Roberta Stanwood appeared happily distracted with pleasant thoughts. As for Sir Thomas, he still expressed disapproval that Theodosia intended to spend so much of her time nursing Stanwood, but he too appeared content to amuse himself for the day.

"I shall take a, er, short ride, I think," he told Theodosia gravely. Then, out of politeness, he turned to Helena and added, "Should you like to accompany me, my dear?"

Rather hastily Helena replied, "No! That is, thank you, Sir Thomas, but I have, er, errands to do about the house."

Holwell then turned to Miss Roberta Stanwood. "I understand you do not care for horses, or I should invite you."

Cousin Roberta shuddered delicately. "Oh, dear me, no, I do not care for the creatures. It is the one thing, Nella, that upset your grandfather about me. No, no, don't worry about me. I have more than enough to occupy me here."

She turned to Theodosia, and for a moment it seemed as though she would speak. But she did not, and Theodosia could only be thankful, for it appeared she would escape the scold she knew Miss Stanwood ought to deliver. So Theodosia held her own counsel, watching Holwell and wondering if he had indeed struck Stanwood over the head or whether there was someone else at work. Someone who was not content merely to steal the strongbox and attack Stanwood, but who wished as well to cast the blame on others.

Immediately after breakfast Helena caught up with Theodosia in the hallway and said, "Dosie, Peter is coming over to help us look for the hidden treasure today! Isn't that marvelous? I know we ought to be thinking of Bartram, but you are doing that, and meantime, Peter and I shall see what we can find."

"Mr. Cranley?" Theodosia asked in surprise.

"Yes! He seems certain we can find it," Helena confided breathlessly. "He says we need only look for hollow walls or consult old plans to see where a secret room might have been hidden. What fun he and I shall have today! And you, as well, if you can tear yourself away from my brother's side."

"I cannot join the search today," Theodosia said at last. "I am needed in the stillroom. But you and Mr. Cranley can manage well enough alone, I am certain."

Helena hesitated; then propriety overcame excitement. "You are right, of course. But it does seem a shame you must miss all the fun. Still, you shall be the first to know if we find anything."

"Good," Theodosia told her friend firmly. Then, noticing Helena's dress for the first time, she said slowly, "Do you know, Nella, I cannot but think that for such work an old morning dress would do better than sprigged muslin. Where and when did you get it?"

Helena gazed at her friend innocently. "Bartram did say I might have a new dress, and there is a Mrs. Caldwell in the village who does excellent work with her needle at very reasonable prices."

Theodosia frowned. "But I should not have thought there had been time for her to make a dress. Wasn't it just a day or two ago that Bartram said you might order one?"

Helena blushed. "Well . . . I knew he would come about, and I did need a new dress . . ."

"So you contrived to order one as soon as we got here," Theodosia finished the answer for her. She sighed. "Well, it is your own affair, but I still cannot help thinking that you would be better served today by wearing something old. There *are* dusty corners about here."

"Yes, but Peter said he would do all the prying about in dusty places. Besides, how am I to have him notice me if I wear something old?" Helena asked mournfully.

Amused, Theodosia said, "I assume then that you no longer suspect him of prowling about here the other night?"

Indignantly Helena retorted, "He explained all that! He hung about hoping to speak to me. Alone."

"Why not at his sister's party?" Theodosia asked reasonably.

Again Helena blushed. "He could not. His sister would have moved to prevent such a thing. She does not in the least approve of me, you know. Anyway, I cannot believe Peter would ever do anything to hurt Bartram!"

Theodosia wondered how Stanwood would feel about his sister's evident attachment to Peter Cranley. It was not, however, she told herself firmly, her affair. Cousin Roberta had been engaged to act as chaperon to Nella; let her do so. It was therefore with a relatively clear conscience that Theodosia bid her friend good luck and told her to enjoy herself and then went to the stillroom. As she had told Helena, there was much to be done.

It was a couple of hours later before Theodosia ventured up to Stanwood's room. Henry answered her tap at the door with surprising speed. Theodosia soon understood why. A harassed look about him, the poor fellow said, "You convince him, Lady Theodosia, that he must take this medicine."

Theodosia warily eyed the viscount's grimly set face and felt like retreating. But Elstons do not retreat, she told herself firmly, and advanced toward the bed. "Now, what's this all about?" she asked briskly.

"I won't take any more of that quack's potions, powders, or cordials," Stanwood told her irritably.

Briefly Theodosia turned back to the valet and said, "I think you'd best leave this to me, Henry."

With relief the poor fellow bowed and withdrew. Then Theodosia regarded her patient, looking carefully at his coloring, checking his pulse, and feeling his forehead for fever. When she was done she nodded. "Very well," she said coolly, "no more potions, powders, or cordials unless you choose to take them."

So astonished was the viscount that he sat bolt upright in bed and said, "What?"

In spite of herself, Theodosia chuckled. "It's quite all right, I assure you. My brother once hurt his head, much like you did, except that his was in a fall from a horse. At the time, the nursing fell to me, and our doctor told me that after the first day or so, such medicines are best forgotten so long as the patient will behave himself and remain quiet. You will promise to do so, I trust?" Stanwood hesitated and Theodosia added, "You needn't worry about the treasure. Nella and Peter Cranley are busy looking for hollow walls and possible hidden rooms right now."

"Indeed?" Stanwood's voice was mocking. "And while my charming impostor plays the nurse, what does her accomplice do?"

Theodosia felt herself stiffen. With scarcely suppressed anger she said, "If you mean Sir

Thomas, he has gone out riding. As I said, you
need have no fear. And now I shall call your valet.
I have no doubt you would prefer his company."

Immediately Stanwood's hand shot out to stop
her. "Oh, no," he said in a low, serious voice,
"I've no intention of letting you go just yet!"

"What . . . what do you mean?" Theodosia demanded.

The viscount shrugged, and his voice was light
but he did not let go Theodosia's hand as he said,
"Why, surely you can understand that I scarcely
dare let you out of my sight. You might go after
the treasure yourself."

Angrily Theodosia tried to free her hand, but
the viscount's grip was surprisingly strong.
Flushed, she told him, "You cannot know how
much I wish I were quit of this place and back in
Bath so that I need never see your face again!"

"Indeed?" Stanwood retorted. "You did not
seem so indifferent to me yesterday."

At the reference to his kiss and her response,
Theodosia blushed deeper, and it was at that
moment that Miss Roberta Stanwood choose to
enter the room, without knocking at the door
first. "Good heavens!" she gasped. "Not again?
My dear Lady Theodosia, I really must remon-
strate with you. You cannot go on behaving this
way! The impropriety of it all. Just the question
of your spending so much time alone with a
gentleman who is not of your family. And in his
bedroom. To say nothing of the behavior I witnessed yesterday. I do not know what your

grandmother would say if she knew how I have betrayed the trust she placed in me, allowing me to chaperon you here."

Miss Stanwood might have gone on for some time had Stanwood not cut her short by saying innocently, "But, Cousin Roberta, what impropriety can there be? Lady Theodosia and I are betrothed, and therefore it is perfectly all right for her to nurse me."

It is difficult to say who went more pale, then colored more deeply at the viscount's words. Certainly Miss Stanwood recovered her voice first. "Betrothed! Whatever will Miss Cranley say? And Lady Theodosia's grandmother? Dear, dear, this is all so . . . so unexpected. Why?"

A voice cut in sharply from behind Miss Stanwood. "You need not concern yourself with what Miss Cranley will say, for I am right here." Clarissa pushed around Roberta to enter the room. Her face was pale but she retained her composure admirably. "Is this true, Bartram?" she asked quietly. His eyes held hers for several long moments, and he did not deny it. "I see. May I ask why?"

Still holding Theodosia's wrist, Stanwood shrugged. Carelessly he said, "Perhaps I have quite given up hope of finding Grandfather's treasure and I need some way to recoup my family's fortune. And Lady Theodosia will, I understand, bring me a handsome dowry. She is a trifle heedless, I will allow, but I have no doubt I shall soon school her to obedience."

Theodosia shot Stanwood a glowering look, but the viscount was not in the least abashed. Again Miss Stanwood fluttered, "I suppose so, but what about Miss Cranley? She was to have a handsome settlement also, if she married you."

Clarissa half-turned to Roberta and said, "Thank you for that, Miss Stanwood."

With his free hand Stanwood pressed his forehead. "And to think I had forgotten! Ah, well, what's done is done. I am engaged to Lady Theodosia."

"Is this true?" Roberta demanded of Theodosia. "Whatever will I tell your grandmother? And you, Miss Cranley, to come to visit Lord Stanwood and have to deal with this! You must be quite overcome."

Coolly Clarissa replied, "You need not fear that I shall be overcome by a fit of the vapors, Miss Stanwood. This is not, I will allow, what I expected, but I am made of sterner stuff than to faint. Nor am I entirely convinced this nonsense is true. The tale is altogether too foolish to credit."

Theodosia had been about to deny it all, but Miss Cranley's words stopped her. A sense of giddiness seized her, and a desire to shake however briefly, Clarissa Cranley's absolute self-assurance. Taking a deep breath and reminding herself that she was, after all, an Elston, she said demurely, "My dear Miss Stanwood, do you think his lordship would lie to you?"

"But what about Miss Cranley?" Roberta repeated.

Theodosia looked Clarissa in the eye and said firmly, "I take leave to tell Miss Cranley that his lordship is allowed no visitors just yet."

"But about the betrothal?" Roberta wailed.

"I shall tell her that Lady Theodosia's nursing won my heart," Stanwood replied with a grin.

"Miss Cranley is not amused," Clarissa said coldly. "Lady Theodosia, I wish you joy of your marriage. If there is a marriage. Recollect that I too believed myself to have an understanding with his lordship, and you have seen me cast off just now. Beware that it does not happen to you. Good day, Stanwood. Need I say that I am disappointed in you?"

Still shaking her head and fluttering helplessly, Roberta followed Clarissa out of the room. As soon as they were gone, Theodosia rounded on Stanwood and said, "Have you taken leave of your senses, Lord Stanwood?"

"You did not contradict me," Stanwood pointed out mischievously.

"I . . . I could not," Theodosia stammered. "It is never good to upset a patient."

"A wise policy," he agreed, and pulled her closer. Somehow Theodosia found that she did not want to resist. "I've no doubt Clarissa is furious," Stanwood went on, "but what of Holwell? How will he feel?"

Theodosia did not immediately answer, and Stanwood caught her chin with his free hand and

made her look at him. Concerned, he searched her
eyes for some clue as to how she was feeling.
"What is it?" he asked, his voice treacherously
kind. "Did you really mean to marry the fellow? I
know that he meant to marry you, but I had
thought you had more sense than to agree. It
wouldn't have done, you know."

Theodosia shook her head. "No, I never meant
to marry at all. I had no use for such shackles. It
is my grandmother I am worried about. What if
your cousin writes to her and tells her that I am
betrothed to you?"

The viscount slipped a comforting arm about
her waist. "Marry me," he said reasonably, "and
there is no difficulty that I can see."

Angrily Theodosia pulled free and hastily
retreated to a safe distance from the bed. "Now
you are roasting me!" she told him sharply. "You
cannot wish to marry me. You believe I stole the
strongbox from your room and that I am engaged
in some plot to steal this mythical treasure from
you."

The viscount waved a hand airily. "Ah, but as I
told Cousin Roberta, I have no doubt that I can
soon school you to proper obedience. You shan't
cause me any trouble, I am sure."

Speaking very clearly, Theodosia said, "You
may go straight to the devil, Lord Stanwood!"

She turned to go, but Stanwood's voice halted
her. "Wait! You wish the truth? Very well. I do
not like to be pressed into marriage, and the
Cranleys have been trying to do so. At the dinner
party both Clarissa and her father took care to

tell me they expected a declaration within the week."

"And you think it better to have the world believe you are betrothed to me?" Theodosia gasped in astonishment.

For the first time Stanwood looked away. Frowning, he said, "In point of fact, I do. All logic tells me I ought to throw you out of my house, and all instinct tells me I ought to embrace you."

"And this is your compromise?" Theodosia demanded, still incredulous.

He grinned. "At least Clarissa Cranley will no longer be pressing me to marry her."

"And what of me?" Theodosia asked with a lightness she did not feel.

Stanwood met her eyes this time. "If I discover I am mistaken in my suspicions, I shall wed you happily, when and where you will. If I am not, then I shall have no hesitation in breaking it off." Troubled, Theodosia continued to stare at the viscount, until finally he said, again with treacherous kindness, "And now it is your turn. Why did you accept my tale to Cousin Roberta?"

"Because," she said distinctly, "I should prefer not to see you make such a mistake as to marry Clarissa Cranley. Nor to have my reputation ruined by tales she might spread if she knew how much time I have spent in this room, innocent as that time has been. As for the future, however, you needn't worry about breaking off our . . . engagement. I have no doubt I shall do that soon enough. And now, I have other matters to attend to. I shall see you later."

Before he could object, Theodosia turned on her heel and retreated as fast as decorum would allow.

21

To her confusion, Theodosia encountered Helena and Cranley almost as soon as she had left Stanwood's room. Immediately Helena pounced on her. "Are you really going to marry my brother?"

Peter Cranley was more discreet and pulled the pair of them into the nearest empty room. He, too, however, had questions. "Miss Stanwood said that you were betrothed to Lord Stanwood, Lady Theodosia. Is that true? Because if it is, I must warn you that my sister will not accept the matter easily. She expected to be his wife, you know."

Nothing more was wanted to stiffen Theodosia's resolve. It was rare that she took such an instant dislike to someone, but this time she had. Taking a deep breath, Theodosia said, "I did not contradict Stanwood when he told Miss Stanwood that we were betrothed. If your sister is distressed, then I am sorry, Mr. Cranley."

"Well, I'd best go see to her," he said with a shrug. "She'll be in the devil's own temper. Though I must allow that you and Stanwood are far better suited than my sister and he would have been. Nella, I shall help you search some more shortly."

Then he was gone, and Nella turned to Theodosia. "Tell me everything! How did he propose? What made him come up to scratch? When is the wedding to be? What will your grandmother say?"

To Helena's surprise, Theodosia promptly dissolved into tears. "Nella," she gasped, "I want so much to marry your brother, but I fear I am mad to do so! He hates me!"

"How can that be?" Helena retorted reasonably. "He has asked you to marry him."

"No, he has not," Theodosia answered. "He has told your Cousin Roberta we are betrothed, and that is entirely a different matter."

"I don't see how," Helena replied. "My brother is a gentleman and would consider such a pronouncement as binding as any."

"But I don't want him to be bound by such nonsense if he truly despises me," Theodosia protested. "And he said that he did. He calls me an impostor and believes that it is I—or I working with sir Thomas—who bashed him over the head!"

Alarmed, Helena forced her friend to take a chair. Then she felt Theodosia's forehead. "You don't seem feverish," Helena said at last. "But it all sounds mad. How can Bartram suspect you of such a thing? And what does he mean by impostor? Surely he has not guessed that you were the one pretending to be him that day in Bath?"

With an effort, Theodosia forced herself to answer coherently. "No. At least, I think he has not. Oh, Nella, it seems mad to me as well. No less my acceptance of his words to your cousin Roberta and Clarissa Cranley than his speaking them! Your brother despises me, and yet he seems determined to pretend we are betrothed. I love him and yet am convinced it would be madness to truly wed him when he feels so about me. And yet I had not the resolve to deny to Clarissa or your cousin Roberta or Peter Cranley that we are engaged."

For several moments Helena paced the room. At last she came over and knelt beside her friend. "I shall go and speak to Bartram," she said with sudden resolve. "Whatever his reasons, I cannot believe he despises you, or that if he did, he would say he was betrothed to you. He simply does not act in such a way."

Without much hope, Theodosia nodded. "I shall wait here. I cannot bear to go downstairs and encounter Clarissa Cranley again, or Sir Thomas, just now."

"An excellent notion," Helena agreed stoutly. "Wait here, and I shall be back in just a few minutes, I promise you."

While she waited, Theodosia looked around the room for the first time. It was one of the ones Helena had shown her on the tour of the house,

and one of the few with holland covers over all the
furnishings. It seemed a kind of upstairs library,
albeit a very small one, and furnished with little
other than a few solid chairs and one matching
desk made of oak. The cream-colored walls,
however, were lined with bookshelves filled with
books, and idly Theodosia began glancing at
titles. They seemed all jumbled up in no
particular order, and on every variety, from
geography to the wildest of fantasies. To her
surprise, Theodosia found one that appeared not
even to have a title. She was about to take it
down and examine it when the door opened
behind her. It was Helena, and all thoughts of
books promptly fled.

"Well?" Theodosia demanded.

Helena shrugged helplessly. "I can get nothing
out of him," she said. "He is determined to carry
through this pretense for the moment, and I see
no way to dissuade him. If the doctor had not
reassured me it was otherwise, I should suspect
the knock on the head addled my brother's wits."
She hesitated, then added, "In fact, I should
wonder if it addled your wits as well. I have never
known you not to know your own mind before. If
you've a *tendre* for my brother, why not wed him
and be done with the matter?"

Before Theodosia could answer, there was a
soft knock at the door and Peter Cranley poked in
his head. "I think," he said grimly, "you'd best
come downstairs. My sister is making wild state-
ments and threats to tell the world Lady Theodosia has duped your brother, Nella. Someone

had better say something to cool her temper."

Theodosia and Helena looked at one another, then nodded decisively. "Very well, we shall be down directly," Helena said, her voice calmer than either young woman felt.

Peter Cranley had not exaggerated his sister's temper. She was pacing rapidly back and forth in the morning room when Theodosia and Helena entered. Sir Thomas was standing by the far window watching her, concern etched deeply on his face. Miss Stanwood sat in a corner, a look of intense unhappiness about her.

As Theodosia entered, Clarissa turned on her and said with surprising calm, "Is it true, then? Are you to marry Stanwood? Or were the pair of you roasting me upstairs?"

As their eyes met, Theodosia found herself suddenly sympathetic to the young woman facing her. And yet she could not back down. "We have not yet talked of a wedding date," she replied gently, "but—"

"But you are betrothed," Clarissa cut in bitterly. "It is no more than I expected. How is a country family such as mine to compare with the Elstons? Or my portion to compare with that of such a notable heiress? Well, Lady Theodosia, I pray that you have not deluded yourself into believing he marries you out of love! Not that that is the best foundation for a marriage, in any event."

At this point Holwell spoke. "Quite true, Miss Cranley. Mutual esteem, a certain companionable agreement of tastes, a shared sense of what is right and proper—these are essential to the success of a marriage. Not some absurd emotion called love." Holwell paused, then went on, "Lady Theodosia, while I cannot say I consider the match a suitable one, it is not my place to decide such things for you. At the same time, I do, of course, extend to you my wishes for a happy future." He paused again and turned to Clarissa. "Miss Cranley, I know that it cannot be other than painful for you to be here now. May I escort you back home?"

"I am capable of finding my own way," Clarissa replied gamely.

He bowed. "Of course you are. I thought, however, that a sympathetic companion might help. You are, after all, not the only one to suffer disappointment today. Though I venture to say that we will not always feel so."

Clarissa met Holwell's eyes and, after a moment, graciously inclined her head. "I should be glad of your company. Indeed I must admit I find myself in need of a wiser head than mine at such a time," she said in a voice gentler than Theodosia had heard her use before. "Lady Theodosia, Helena, I pray you will excuse me. I am in no temper for polite conversation today. Good day to both of you. And to you as well, Peter, since it appears you choose to remain in this household without regard to how I have been insulted."

Without waiting for any more to be said, Clarissa swept out of the room, with Holwell at her side, leaving Helena and Theodosia to collapse into nearby chairs in relief. Peter Cranley merely shook his head. "I don't understand it," he said, "but I must say I think your brother, Helena, had a narrow escape. Clarissa is my sister and I ought not to say this, but I have never thought they would suit."

"Nor I." Helena nodded grimly.

To everyone's astonishment, Roberta spoke up. With a sniff she said, "You are unfeeling, the pair of you. Indeed, all three of you. *You* cannot know, or care I suppose, what it is like to be told that the man who was to marry you has chosen to wed another! Well, I wash my hands of the lot of you." Rising to her feet, Miss Stanwood moved toward the door, not troubling to hide her distress as she mumbled, "I must go. I have letters I must write at once."

For a moment there was silence as they watched her go. Then Peter Cranley said cheerfully, "Well, that's over with—the tears and tantrums, I mean. Now what do we do?"

"What do we do *now?*" Helena demanded in shocked indignation. "We go on looking for a secret hiding place, or had you forgotten?"

"Did you look for the original floor plans of the house?" Theodosia asked mildly.

Peter Cranley frowned. "Yes, we did, but they are nowhere to be found. So we are reduced to pacing rooms to see if dimensions match, and sounding walls for hollow places."

"Well, I wish you luck," Theodosia said with a sigh. "I have to return to the sickroom."

"Scarcely a hardship, under the circumstances,

I should think," Cranley observed, a twinkle in his eyes.

Theodosia laughed. "If you saw my patient, you would not say so! He may have offered for my hand, but that makes him no more agreeable when he is told he must still remain in bed and eat an invalid's meals."

22

The following week passed quietly enough, a circumstance for which Theodosia was grateful. Clarissa Cranley came no more to the Oaks and Sir Thomas spent a great deal of time on his own. Or so Theodosia thought until Peter Cranley reported he was a frequent visitor at the Cranley household. Why Sir Thomas did not simply leave Stanwood Oaks and return to Bath or London, or at the very least an inn (if he wished to remain in the neighborhood to visit the Cranleys), was another matter altogether, and one beyond Theodosia's comprehension. Peter Cranley's theory was that Holwell was after the hidden fortune, still wishing, of course, to avenge family honor. Unless, of course, he was merely short on funds. Helena was inclined to agree, but Miss Roberta Stanwood was appalled at such speculation.

As for Stanwood himself, he kept his thoughts hidden. His health continued to improve slowly but steadily, and Theodosia continued to give

false reports. She could not shake the fear that if
it were known how well his lordship was progress-
ing, there might be another attack. He was un-
failingly polite to Theodosia but spoke no further
on the subject of marriage, nor did he send a
notice to any of the London papers. Instead their
conversations were limited to domestic matters
and his health. It was, Theodosia could not help
feeling, rather like an uneasy truce between them.
Fortunately, there had not been a letter from
Grandmama, and Theodosia allowed herself the
hope that Miss Stanwood had not chosen to write
to her of the supposed betrothal after all.

It was precisely a week after the attack when
Stanwood asked abruptly, "How goes the
progress on finding my grandfather's fortune?"
Theodosia looked at him blankly, and he went on
impatiently, "My sister and that Cranley puppy.
How goes their search for the fortune?"

"How did you know about that?" Theodosia
could not help but ask.

Stanwood paced about the room in his dressing
gown. He had been up and out of bed for several
days now, but Theodosia and the valet were the
only ones privy to the secret. He turned and
looked at her. "You were the one who first men-
tioned it to me. And in any event, Henry tells me
a great deal," he said dryly. "I gather I am to
look for an engagement in that direction before
too long?"

Theodosia looked down at the needlework in
her hands, trying to hide her confusion. "Would
you be displeased if there were?" she parried.

"No. I should not care to marry the sister, but young Cranley is a likeable fellow and will make Nella a decent husband. I've no doubt they will forever be in one scrape or another, but they shall be happy," Stanwood replied. "As will Holwell and Clarissa."

"Holwell and Clarissa?" Theodosia asked, once more startled.

Stanwood knit his brows together, frowning. "Didn't you know?" he asked. "I was sure you must, since he is forever going over there."

"I suppose I had." Theodosia nodded. "I simply didn't think forward to what it might mean."

Stanwood crossed the room to stand over Theodosia. "Are you distressed?" he demanded bluntly. "When I told Cousin Roberta we were to be betrothed, I knew Holwell would turn elsewhere for comfort. Ought I to apologize to you for that? I warn you I cannot say I feel sorry for it; it would never have done, you know, for you to marry the fellow."

Theodosia set aside her needlework. With a sigh she said, "I wonder at times if it will ever do for me to marry anyone. I shall not make the easiest of wives, and I find I am rather fussy when it comes to the men who might have offered for me."

"I ought then to feel flattered you have agreed to marry me," Stanwood observed lightly.

Theodosia flushed and looked up, her eyes locking with Stanwood's. "But you didn't really mean it," she protested. "You cannot, when you

think me behind the attack on you. And you've
not said a word this past week about the matter. I
thought . . ."

"You thought I had changed my mind?" Stanwood asked, his tone still light. Theodosia
nodded, and he bent down and pulled her to her
feet, his arms imprisoning her about the waist.
"Do you think me so given to passing fancies,
then?" he asked. "Or is the notion of marriage to
me so repugnant to you that you merely wish
that I would give up the notion?"

Theodosia tried to break free, but he would not
let her. "You are mad," she flung at him. "I
thought your words last week a product of the
blow on the head and that they would soon be forgotten."

"But they are not," Stanwood replied easily.
"And I ask again, do you find me repugnant?"

In desperation she said, "You know nothing
about me! I did not help to hurt you, nor have any
part of such a plan. But I am not as you think.
You have called me an impostor . . . well, so I was,
in Bath. It was I who dressed as a man and pretended to be you, so that Helena could get out of
the house without her cousin Roberta. I was
Devere."

For a moment Stanwood was startled, but he
recovered quickly. "Well, that is one admirer of
my sister's that I need not worry about then. And
I've no doubt you made a charming fellow. But
what is that to the purpose? Unless you have
somehow conceived a distaste for me and wish to

spare my feelings by telling such tales so I will break off the betrothal."

With one hand Stanwood tilted up Theodosia's chin and forced her to look at him. Her eyes met his and filled treacherously. She found words tumbling out that she had never meant to say. "I will not marry a man who despises me, no matter how I feel! I've seen too much of uneven marriages to wed where I only care. You said last week you could not live without me, but how long before contempt conquers need and you hate the chains that bind us together? I will not do that to the two of us, I will not!"

But Stanwood's ears had heard the other, more important words she said. "You do not hate me, then?" he asked. "You are not even indifferent?"

Theodosia did not answer, but she did not have to—the answers were evident in her eyes. Before she knew what he was about, Stanwood had swept her into his arms and brought his lips down on hers. He had not touched her in a week, and the warmth she had felt then overwhelmed her now. No reminders of propriety, no thoughts of convention could keep her from responding to his kisses. It was he who broke off first.

"We shall be married," he said quietly, "as soon as we are able. My love will not turn to hate, nor yours."

"But Clarissa . . ." Theodosia found the words to protest. "I am nothing like her."

Gently Stanwood let go of Theodosia and stepped back and once more spoke lightly.

"Thank heaven for that! I've no wish to be married to her or someone like her."

Theodosia frowned. "So you said last week. But you have forever been telling Nella and me that you did want someone like her. Someone sober and serious who could help you make something of your family estate again."

"So I thought." Stanwood nodded. "I had everything planned out and decided. Then you entered my life, posing first as a little Puritan, than a giddy girl, then a fashion plate, then . . . then I don't know what. And I suddenly knew I could not live with a marble statue like Clarissa. I needed someone alive and willful and unexpected. Just like you."

He started to reach for her again, when there was a knock at the door. The two looked at one another and Stanwood hastily climbed back into the bed. A moment later Theodosia opened the door. It was Helena and Peter, both terribly excited. "We've figured it out!" Peter crowed.

"Oh?" Stanwood asked with a yawn. "Figured what out?"

"Where the room must be!" Cranley retorted indignantly.

"It's in the upstairs bookroom," Helena said excitedly. "The one next to your bedroom. We've paced out all the rooms, and that's where it must be!"

Gone was Stanwood's languid manner as he replied, pushing aside the covers, "Show me!"

If Helena and Cranley were surprised to see Bartram climb so easily out of bed, they said nothing; instead they eagerly led the way. Theodosia followed, shaking her head slightly and wondering if they would all soon find themselves in Bedlam.

Helena pushed open the door to the bookroom and halted in astonishment. They all did. For there was Cousin Roberta with a bookshelf pushed aside, fumbling at a door that had been hidden behind it!

23

"Cousin Roberta! What the devil are you doing here?" Stanwood exclaimed.

Startled, she stood upright and fluttered her hands. "Oh, dear, I, er, the door was open and I came in and found the, er, bookcase . . ."

But Helena had already stridden forward and wrenched a piece of paper out of Miss Stanwood's weak grasp. "It's what you found in the strongbox," she told Bartram. "At least I think so."

Stanwood held out his hand imperatively and Helena placed the paper in it. He glanced quickly at Helena's find, then nodded. "You're right, Nella. Tell me, Cousin Roberta, how do you come to have this?"

For a moment the lady stared at him; then, almost, she seemed to grow taller. Angrily she said, "How do I come to have it? I have it because I deserve it! It was unthinkable to your grandfather to leave a mere girl more than a pittance, but I *was* his favorite niece! His favorite relative,

I should guess, and he left nothing to me, nothing of real importance. Certainly not enough to live on. I was to support myself by staying with relatives and friends year round, for that was what spinsters like myself do!" Miss Stanwood fairly spat out the words, nor did her tone moderate as she went on, "It was because of him I never married, you know. Somehow, every time someone seemed about to offer for me, your grandfather was there and the gentleman never did. He needed me, you see. I spent more time here than in my own home.

"I was the one your grandfather confided in. I was the one who listened to all his stories. I was the one who believed in his worth! But did he care? Oh, no, I was only a girl. So he hid his treasure and told me to tell you about it one day, and so I did. Knowing you would find the clues to where the treasure was hidden. And then I would claim it. For that is still what I intend to do. It is mine! Or should be, in a more just world. I deciphered the last directions and I found the door to the treasure room. I should have even had the keys, had you not awakened, Stanwood, and startled me before I could find them!"

The viscount's eyes met Theodosia's and he colored. "So it was you who struck me?" he asked Roberta.

She nodded. "But I didn't mean to hurt you so badly," she said querulously. "I just wanted the keys. It was the same with Jeremy, you know. I never meant for him to slip and fall. But when he came to me for stories and then went looking for the treasure, I didn't want to stop him. He must have found the journal in the library, but I didn't know that. He never told me, you see, how far along he was in the search. He never told anyone."

Stanwood had slowly moved forward until he stood directly in front of Miss Stanwood. Now he set her aside and pulled the keys from the pocket of his robe. "I doubt you would have found the keys," he told her quietly, "for I had them well hidden, *not* under my pillow. This is the door they fit, I presume?"

"Yes, of course it is!" Roberta flung at him. "But it's my treasure, I tell you, and I will have it!"

Stanwood inserted the key and turned it, the lock protesting with age, as he replied, "No, Miss Stanwood, it is not your treasure. This is not a fair world, and you have already told me that Grandfather meant me to have the inheritance. No doubt to keep up the estate, for you have said he knew my father would bring us to the edge of financial ruin. But you are right, he should have provided for you, and so I shall do as soon as I have ascertained how great the funds will be."

"Provide for me?" Roberta Stanwood demanded in disbelief. "Be dependent upon your charity? I will not have it! I want to be wealthy. To live in London as your mother and father did. I want to order gowns from the best dressmakers in the world and buy myself presents from the most expensive jewelers! I will not live on mere charity."

By now Stanwood had the door open and they all crowded forward to look, Stanwood allowing his father's cousin Roberta to precede him. Light came from the candles Theodosia had providently lit as soon as she saw that the keys would work, and she handed them around to everyone there. Even Miss Roberta Stanwood was overwhelmed by what she saw. "I . . . I had no notion there was so much or that it was so beautiful," she whispered.

Stanwood turned to her. "Beautiful? So it is. Would you truly have me sell it all for mere wealth? I should rather put it on display and sell only what I must for all our needs."

"He was so rich!" Roberta went on as if she had not heard. "And yet he did not live as if he were."

"No, he did not," Stanwood agreed. "Perhaps he felt no need, secure in his own house and knowing what he had and what he had done."

"But he lied to me!" she hissed. "I wanted to see his treasure, and he said there was nothing he could show me. That it was too well hidden away. That I would not have liked it anyway. A simple jade pin he gave me, but what do I see here? Jade statues and bowls, enamel work beyond anything to be found in London, silk, brocade, embroidered cloth, vases, urns, chest of precious things! Nothing to show me? I cannot believe he was so cruel."

Miss Stanwood turned and quietly fled the room. No one saw her go, for they were all too busy examining the treasures. Stanwood was the first to speak. "Well," he said, "my grandfather was indeed a traveler to China, it seems, and he did indeed bring back a treasure. I can only be grateful my parents had no wind of it. I shudder to think how much *they* might have sold off."

Hesitantly Helena said, "Do you think, Bartram, we might sell off just enough to give me a marriage portion?"

Stanwood's eyes met Peter Cranley's. "No," the viscount said quietly, "I do not intend to do so. Somehow I think your future husband, whoever he may be, would accept a part of these treasures as your portion and not demand pounds sterling."

"I should think so!" Cranley echoed fervently.

Helena sighed. "Good. I was rather regretting the need to sell anything. It's all so beautiful!"

Just then they heard voices in the bookroom behind them, and Stanwood called out, "We are in here!"

A moment later Clarissa Cranley and Sir Thomas Holwell joined them. Clarissa held up her skirts and wrinkled her nose a trifle in distaste. "It is so dusty in here," she said, backing out again.

The others followed her out as Helena shot back, "Yes, but so wealthy."

Hastily Sir Thomas intervened. "I just came . . . that is . . . we just came," he said, "to inform you that Miss Cranley and I are engaged to be married. While neither of us is inclined to undue haste, we have set a date three months from today. I trust that will give us sufficient time for all the announcements and preparations that will be required. Meanwhile I shall be removing myself from your hospitality, Lord Stanwood, and returning to London to have my solicitors draw up the necessary papers."

Placing a proprietary arm around Theodosia's waist, Stanwood replied, "We wish you Godspeed and all future happiness."

"Amen," Theodosia added fervently.

Clarissa inclined her head graciously. "Thank you, Lady Theodosia. We have not, I know, always agreed, and I confess to having had, at times, uncharitable thoughts toward you. But now that Sir Thomas and I are to be wed, I must tender you my thanks for having brought him here to our neighborhood, for otherwise I should never have met him. And I, too, wish both of you happiness."

For the first time Peter spoke up. "Well, I must say that this is not entirely unexpected and that I am quite certain you will suit each other perfectly."

"How very kind of you," Holwell answered, surprised. "I had no notion you approved of my suit."

Clarissa, who knew her brother rather better than Sir Thomas did, immediately said, "Yes, well, perhaps we'd best be going. You must pack and I have other errands to attend to, Sir Thomas."

"Of course, my dear," he agreed. They started to leave the room; then Holwell paused to ask, "By the by, what the devil was wrong with your cousin Miss Stanwood? We encountered her outside the room and she brushed past us, extremely distressed, and told us you were in here."

"A, er, disagreement over the, er, disposition of my grandfather's legacy," Stanwood offered vaguely.

Holwell nodded. "That all? Was a bit worried, but females can be such watering pots. That sort especially. Well, good day, and thank you again for your hospitality, Stanwood."

Then, offering her his arm, Holwell left the room with Clarissa, leaving Helena and Peter to dissolve in whoops of laughter as soon as they were gone.

"Now, now," Stanwood said, trying to speak sternly, "you ought to have more respect for your sister, Cranley."

"But I do," Peter protested between gasps of breath. "A great deal of respect for both of them. So much so that I shall dance very happily at their wedding and see them off to their new home, far away from here, with genuine pleasure. They are, without doubt, the most respectable couple I have ever seen!"

Once more he and Helena laughed, and Stanwood shrugged helplessly. Instead of trying to talk further to the pair, he turned, and making sure there were no candles left inside the room, closed and locked the door that led to the treasure. To Theodosia he said quietly, "I shall have to have someone come in and study what is in there before I know what this treasure is worth, but I have no doubt that I am no longer a pauper." He paused as though lost in thought, but finally went on, "My grandfather must have been a strange fellow. Someday I shall show you his journals. Few men have half the adventures he encountered, and fewer still live to tell about them. So many beautiful things so carefully hidden, I cannot altogether comprehend it."

"What about your father's cousin Roberta?" Theodosia asked hesitantly.

Stanwood raised his eyebrows in surprise. "I meant what I said, of course. I shall provide a yearly stipend for her, once I know what funds are available to me. She is quite right in saying life has been hard for her."

Theodosia nodded and shivered. "I am glad you feel that way. I should not like ever to find myself in her position—it has not been an enviable one. I think I shall go find her, for I cannot help but be troubled by her distress."

"An excellent notion," Stanwood agreed. "I confess I find myself more than a little concerned as to what she may do. I had no notion she was involved in Jeremy's death. And while I believe it may have been his own foolishness that led him to climb where the rocks might fall on him, still . . ."

Theodosia nodded. "Still, it would be best if someone kept an eye on her." She started to go, then paused to ask, "How in God's name could your grandfather have treated her in so heartless a manner?"

"He was not a man given to kindness," Stanwood retorted grimly. "Perhaps he felt he had had little enough of it in his own life. Nor do we have other than my cousin's word for it that he did treat her so heartlessly. Perhaps he had reasons we know nothing of."

Once more Theodosia nodded. "True. At any rate, I had best go and find her."

"Good. I shall dress and meet you downstairs shortly. We have much to talk about, including my absurd suspicions!" Stanwood said quietly.

Theodosia colored and fled the room before he could speak further.

24

Theodosia found Miss Stanwood in the downstairs foyer. A hastily packed bag was at her feet and she was pulling on her gloves. Miss Cranley stood beside her, a look of utter satisfaction upon her face. Miss Stanwood spoke in a quavering voice as she said, "Good-bye, Lady Theodosia. I had hoped to leave without seeing you again. Miss Cranley has kindly consented to drop me at the inn, where I shall be able to hire passage to Bath. No doubt you will wish to make your own arrangements about leaving here, since there will be no one to chaperon you. Certainly I shall call upon your grandmother immediately upon my return to Bath and inform her that you are now here alone. What she will make of that, I do not wish to think."

"What she will make of that," Theodosia answered coolly, "is that you have recklessly abandoned your responsibilities here and that we are making the best of a difficult situation."

"Recklessly abandoned my responsibilities?" Roberta Stanwood demanded angrily. "How can you say that, when you must see that I have no choice!"

Sweetly Clarissa stepped into the conversation. "Never mind, Miss Stanwood, we are all aware of your devotion to duty and that only the most dire circumstances could lead you to abandon your post."

"Frankly, other than a certain degree of embarrassment, I can see no reason for your leaving," Theodosia retorted bluntly. "And that, Miss Stanwood, is soon gotten over, as you have so often told Nella."

"*Mere embarrassment?*" Roberta demanded incredulously. "Is that what you think drives me away? Oh, no, it is the impossibility of facing all of you and knowing that right here in this house is a treasure that might have been mine had I only acted more quickly and more resolutely. Treasure that ought to have been mine had I not been born a girl or had my uncle not had this absurd preference for boys. No, Lady Theodosia, I will not stay here and be constantly reminded of what ought to be mine while I endure on a mere pittance. Come, Miss Cranley, I am ready to go."

Clarissa, whose look of triumph had gone to one of puzzlement, collected herself sufficiently to reply, "Certainly, Miss Stanwood. At once. You will be wanting to discover the earliest coach to London. From there it will be no difficulty to get one to Bath."

Theodosia made one last effort. "Miss Stanwood, I've no doubt his lordship would send you back in one of his own carriages, if you wish. Won't you stay long enough to ask him? I know he wishes to speak with you."

Roberta Stanwood looked at Theodosia with bitterness. "I do not choose to put him to the trouble," she said proudly. "I will not accept charity from him when he has robbed me of what is rightfully mine."

There was, it seemed to Theodosia, no more to be said, and short of physically restraining Miss Stanwood, she could see no way to prevent her from going. And even Theodosia shrank from such a move. She watched as they descended the steps to Clarissa's carriage and her shoulders drooped a trifle as she made the necessary calculations. Three days might be allowed for Miss Stanwood's return to Bath, and by then Theodosia had best be back there herself if she did not wish to see her reputation in shreds. For Theodosia did not doubt there would be plenty of tongues to spread the tale and ruin her if she were not.

Then there was the matter of what was to be done about Miss Stanwood's behavior. Theodosia was not in the least certain Stanwood would be content merely to forget what had occurred. Slowly she turned to go back into the house and tell Stanwood of her failure to stop his cousin Roberta. And arrange for her own departure, she reminded herself. As she was about to do so, however, another carriage swept up the long drive. Dear God, she wondered, what next?

Theodosia's curiosity turned to dread as she recognized the emblem on the coach as it pulled up beside Clarissa's. The coat of arms was that of the Earl of Elston, and Theodosia felt not the least surprise, only dismay, as her brother emerged from it. Nor did the expression upon his face reassure her. He paused to speak to the two ladies, and only then did he start up the steps, his eyes locking grimly with Theodosia's.

"Why, George," she said nervously, "whatever are you doing here?"

Through grimly clenched teeth he replied, "Come, my sister, to give you the happy news that Maria has just this week presented me with a daughter, and come to discover for myself what the devil is going on here! With Mother gone and Grandmother busy with her card games in Bath, it falls to me to see what scrape you have gotten yourself into now. Instead of Bath, you are here— most irregularly—with Grandmama telling me some tangled tale about someone named Devere. Said you impersonated the fellow!"

"On the contrary," Theodosia said with a twinkle in her eyes, "*I* was Devere and I was impersonating Lord Stanwood. And that was in Bath. Oh, George, you would have loved it!"

The earl regarded his sister as though she had gone mad. "That I take leave to doubt," he said. "Matters are far worse than I first believed. I only hope it is still possible for us to retrieve your reputation, Theodosia."

Cold with anger, his sister said, "If you intend to take this tone with me, then I suggest we go inside to speak rather than bandy words here."

Elston bowed and allowed his sister to lead the way. Theodosia chose the drawing room and carefully shut the doors behind her brother. Then she turned to him and said in a voice laden with irony, "Pray have a seat, dear brother. It is so delightful to have a visit from you and to hear of your loving concern for me."

But Elston merely stood, hands on hips, regarding her. "I will not sit," he said curtly. "I am here to discover how much is truth of the farrago of nonsense I have heard about your presence here. Is it true you are unchaperoned?"

"As of just now," Theodosia conceded. "You saw Miss Stanwood as she was leaving. She is, you will recollect, Nella's cousin and had been our chaperon. I was about to go upstairs and make my own preparations to return to Bath. I had not yet done so, however, as her departure was so precipitate."

"And so you are here alone with Lord Stanwood and his sister?" Elston demanded.

"And Sir Thomas Holwell. And quite a few servants, you know," Theodosia added mildly. "Incuding Mrs. Thompson, Stanwood's housekeeper."

"Sir Thomas?" George seemed almost upon the point of apoplexy. "That is true, then? I thought Grandmother had merely confused what Holwell told her."

"Of course he is here," Theodosia replied,

driven now by a mischievous demon. "And has been for some time. He wished, it seems, to spare me from Stanwood's unwelcome attentions."

"Unwelcome attentions?" Elston sputtered. "Stanwood has pressed unwelcome attentions on you?"

"Why, no," Theodosia said innocently. "Sir Thomas merely thought he would. But they were not, you see, unwelcome after all."

Elston eyed his sister with distinct disfavor. "I do not find this a matter for jesting," he said.

Theodosia turned serious. "Why not?" she demanded. "I cannot recall that your behavior was above reproach when you were my age. Indeed, there were any number of scrapes Papa had to bail you out of. So why do you lecture me this way? It is not as though the Elstons do not have a history of trouble. Indeed, compared with Mama, I am a pattern of propriety!"

"It is precisely because our family does have a reputation for recklessness that we must be doubly careful of appearances," Elston said crisply. "My own past does not bear speaking of, but now that I am married, that has changed. I cannot think what Maria will say when she hears this. It is not at all what she is accustomed to."

"Then she ought not to have married into our family!" Theodosia shot back. At the sight of her brother's distressed face, however, Theodosia relented. More gently she said, "I am sorry, George. And I am genuinely fond of Maria. But it is the outside of enough for her—or you—to attempt to dictate my behavior."

"Quite true," a voice said from behind her. "I am the only one with a right to do that."

Theodosia whirled to confront Stanwood. He was fully dressed now, as much a man of fashion as Elston. He bowed to both of them and then addressed George. "Hallo, Elston. It's been a while since we last met, hasn't it?"

His face rigid with disapproval, Elston replied, "I could truthfully say I wish it had been longer."

Stanwood looked from one to the other with raised eyebrows. "Oh, dear," he said, "Theodosia has not yet told you."

"Told me what?" Elston asked warily.

"Why, that we are to be married," Stanwood replied innocently. "We have not yet set a date, it is true."

"Or sent a notice to the papers," Theodosia added helpfully.

"Quite true." He bowed to her. "Nevertheless, we are betrothed."

"You have not yet asked my permission," Elston pointed out coldly.

"Very true. There has not yet been the opportunity," Stanwood conceded, abruptly serious. "We have any number of details to work out: settlements and such."

"I said, you have not yet asked my approval," Elston repeated. "Do you truly think I am eager to see my sister wed to a man whose estate is in such a precarious financial situation?"

Stanwood nodded. "I'd forgotten, you don't know yet. This morning I recouped everything." At Elston's look of disbelief, Stanwood said, "I think you'd best follow me upstairs. It will be far simpler to show you than to try to explain."

"Very well," George agreed, "but I warn you I shall not be easily swayed from looking out for my sister's interests."

"Wait a moment!" Theodosia's desperate voice halted them. Coloring under her brother's disapproving gaze she turned to Stanwood and said, "I've got to tell you—your father's cousin Roberta has left Stanwood Oaks. She is on her way to an inn where she intends to hire passage on a coach to London and from there to Bath. I tried to stop her, but I couldn't."

Oblivious of the angry earl, Stanwood put his arms around Theodosia and drew her to his chest. "Don't worry," he told her gently, "there is time enough to deal with her later. When I've had the solicitors draw up the papers to fix an allowance upon her, then I'll go and see her again. Meantime there is nothing she can do to harm any of us."

At this naive pronouncement the earl snorted. "Nothing, you say?" he demanded. "Just ruin my sister's reputation is all! What do you think the tattleboxes will say when they learn Dosie is here unchaperoned? And that is why the pair of us will be leaving in the morning!"

"That we shall see about," Stanwood said, letting Theodosia go and turning to her brother.

"Meanwhile, I was about to show you something upstairs."

Helplessly Theodosia watched them go, feeling rather as though the thing she wanted most to do in the world was to sit down and cry.

25

Theodosia was in her room, still packing her few boxes, when someone rapped at her door. "Come in," she said hesitantly.

It was Helena and she said in surprise, "Dosie! Whatever are you doing?"

"Packing," Theodosia replied shortly. "Your father's cousin Roberta has left for Bath, *my* brother is here swearing he will not let me marry *your* brother, and I feel as if I am in Bedlam. The only solution that I can see is for me to return to Bath."

Helena sat on the edge of Theodosia's bed and asked bluntly, "Are you so sure Bartram will let you go?"

"What do you mean?" Theodosia asked.

"My brother is a very determined person," Helena answered. "And he means to marry you."

Theodosia set down the clothes in her hands and sat beside her friend. "Even if he does, Nella," she said, "I cannot stay here until the wedding! Not without a chaperon. And in any event, I do not doubt my grandmother will want the wedding in Bath, or my brother will want it at his home, or . . . or someone will say we must wait to see if my mother chooses to return to England for my nuptials as she did for George's. It is only in novels that one decides to wed, does so, and lives happily ever after in twenty pages or less. In real life one must contend with all sorts of absurd details."

"Then you *do* mean to marry Bartram?" Helena asked.

Theodosia nodded. "In spite of my brother or my grandmother or even my mother. But I am too aware of the dangers of gossip to set your brother and myself off on the wrong foot with all of the *ton*. So I must return to Bath before your cousin does. You cannot doubt that she will do whatever is in her power to ruin me. Particularly after today."

"Yes, I do see what you mean," Helena said thoughtfully. "Who would have guessed Cousin Roberta was so . . . so bitter? And Jeremy. I can scarcely credit that it is because of her he is dead. How could we, none of us, have ever noticed what was wrong? Or, indeed, that anything was wrong? Why didn't we see?"

"How many of us ever really looked at her?" Theodosia retorted. "How often do we look at anyone like her? Closely, I mean. If we did, how many elderly spinsters would we find leading such lives of quiet desperation? Her only difference was that she had a hope to hold onto: your grandfather's treasure—and now we have even taken that away from her."

Helena shivered. "When did she leave?"

"When Clarissa did," Theodosia replied wryly, "and so we may expect the tale to be spread from there."

Helena tossed her head. "Well, I shall not regard it. Peter has asked for my hand, and as soon as we can persuade Bartram to come round to accepting the news, we plan to be wed. Even Clarissa won't choose to gossip about her future sister-in-law."

Theodosia was not so certain, but she said nothing. Instead she asked, "Have you seen my brother yet, Nella? Does he seem mellower than when he first arrived?"

"That's what I came to tell you!" Helena said. "Your brother and mine wish to see you downstairs in the drawing room. Right away."

"Have they come to blows yet?" Theodosia asked with a wry smile.

"On the contrary," Helena assured her, "they appear to be the best of friends."

"*That* I find hard to credit!" Theodosia replied.

Nevertheless it was true. The scene that greeted her eyes when she entered the drawing room was one of two men in avid conversation, amiably sharing some wine. The Earl of Elston was the first to see her. "Ah, there you are, Dosie. Stanwood and I have been sketching out the details of your marriage settlement. In spite of everything, you appear to have contracted an advantageous match after all. Maria will be so relieved to hear it—she could not forgive herself for being the cause of your removal from the Season. She will be delighted, simply delighted at the news."

Theodosia looked at Stanwood. "The bookroom upstairs?" she hazarded.

Stanwood grinned. "Yes, I did, er, show your brother my grandfather's legacy. He quite agreed that my family fortunes had improved to the point where I might consider myself an acceptable suitor for an Elston."

"Mind you," Elston broke in at this point to say, "you might have done far better, Dosie. However, there is no denying there is an odd kick to your gallop, and I shall feel better seeing you safely wed. The notion of you of all people dwindling into bloodless spinsterhood does not bear thinking of! Stanwood will do. Everyone will say he married you for your money, of course, but those tattleboxes will quiet down soon enough. Word will spread of his grandfather's legacy, and that will be all right again."

"Word will spread?" Theodosia arched her eyebrows. "Through you, perhaps?"

George shrugged. "Must do something for m'sister," he said. "Mind you, I can't understand why you whistled Holwell down the wind." He paused, then said, "Rather, I can, but Mother won't. For a woman who's never in her life cared a bit about such things for herself, she's dashed ambitious for her children! She'll only remember that Holwell has a larger fortune and better pedigree than Stanwood. But then, you ain't a horse, and I must admit I'd find living with the fellow a trial. No sense of humor, none whatsoever. Better to tie up with a man like Stanwood."

The earl stood and with rare tact added, "Don't doubt you've some talking to do. Dosie, best be ready to leave here in the morning. With Miss Stanwood gone, you can't stay, and neither can I. A new daughter to go back home and see, y'know. Have a notion to take you along with me. Let you see the baby, and then, in a week or so, Stanwood and his sister might come as our guests. But that can be settled later."

And then he very kindly strolled out of the room, taking Helena with him and carefully closing the drawing-room doors behind them. Stanwood looked at Theodosia, who was avoiding his eyes. "I cannot believe my brother has become such a pompous fellow," Theodosia said a trifle breathlessly.

"No, he never had the reputation for it," Stanwood admitted. "In fact, he was quite wild a few years ago."

Theodosia nodded and they both fell silent. For several moments Stanwood waited, watching her. Finally he said, moving closer, "Do you still wish to marry me, Theodosia?"

Theodosia raised her eyes and met his. "Yes," she said very simply.

Stanwood moved closer still. "Even though I was such a fool as to believe you might have tried, with Sir Thomas, to steal my fortune from me?"

"Absurd of me, but I do," Theodosia replied with a grin.

Nothing more was needed for Stanwood to sweep her up in a fierce embrace. "I shall never let you go, never!" he vowed.

When at last Theodosia could catch her breath, she said mischievously, "You shall have to. For a week or so. I am to go with my brother, remember?"

"For a week or so," Stanwood agreed, not lessening in the least his hold on her. "And then I come to claim you: my utterly charming impostor!"

About the Author

April Lynn Kihlstrom was born in Buffalo, New York, and graduated from Cornell University with an M.S. in Operations Research. She, her husband, and their two children enjoy traveling and have lived in Paris, Honolulu, Georgia, and New Jersey. When not writing, April Lynn Kihlstrom enjoys needlework and devotes her time to handicapped children.

Also new from Signet

A DANGEROUS PASSION: DAN'S STORY

by JoAnn Robb

Who *was* Jenny Winslow . . . and why had investigative reporter Dan McGee fallen so hard for this beautiful stranger in top secret trouble? Logic told him that love didn't come from a few days of dodging bullets and a few nights of explosive passion, but for the first time in his footloose life he'd found a woman he could settle down with . . . if her sinister pursuers didn't kill her first. And even if they both got out of this mysterious mess alive, would Dan's modern-day Mata Hari ever hang up her cloak and dagger for good . . . for him. . . ?

☐ 0451-138953 $2.50, U.S./ $2.95, Canada
